They stopped at Tarn Hows.

'This has to be my favourite place,' said Francesca. She was sitting on a large, smooth boulder among ferns whose fresh green stalks pierced the crispness of last year's bracken, their leaves tightly curled, poised to unfurl. 'To me it brings back everything that was good about my childhood.'

'In that case,' murmured Guy, putting his arm round her, drawing her close, 'maybe it should be here that I tell you that I've fallen in love with you.'

Laura MacDonald lives in the Isle of Wight. She is married and has a grown-up family. She has enjoyed writing fiction since she was a child, but for several years she worked for members of the medical profession, both in pharmacy and in general practice. Her daughter is a nurse and has helped with the research for Laura's medical stories.

Recent titles by the same author:

THE DECIDING FACTOR
IN AT THE DEEP END
STRICTLY PROFESSIONAL
TO LOVE AGAIN

TOTAL RECALL

BY
LAURA MACDONALD

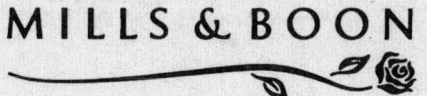

DID YOU PURCHASE THIS BOOK WITHOUT A COVER?
If you did, you should be aware it is **stolen property** as it was reported *unsold and destroyed* by a retailer. Neither the Author nor the publisher has received any payment for this book.

All the characters in this book have no existence outside the imagination of the author, and have no relation whatsoever to anyone bearing the same name or names. They are not even distantly inspired by any individual known or unknown to the author, and all the incidents are pure invention.

All rights reserved. The text of this publication or any part thereof may not be reproduced or transmitted in any form or by any means, electronic or mechanical, including photocopying, recording, storage in an information retrieval system, or otherwise, without the written permission of the publisher.

This book is sold subject to the condition that it shall not, by way of trade or otherwise, be lent, resold, hired out or otherwise circulated without the prior consent of the publisher in any form of binding or cover other than that in which it is published and without a similar condition including this condition being imposed on the subsequent purchaser.

MILLS & BOON, the Rose Device and
LOVE ON CALL are trademarks of the publisher.
Harlequin Mills & Boon Limited,
Eton House, 18-24 Paradise Road, Richmond, Surrey TW9 1SR
This edition published by arrangement with Harlequin Enterprises B.V.

© Laura MacDonald 1996

ISBN 0 263 79459 8

Set in Times 10 on 10 pt. by
Rowland Phototypesetting Limited
Bury St Edmunds, Suffolk

03-9601-53022

Made and printed in Great Britain
Cover illustration by Alexis Liosatos

CHAPTER ONE

IT WAS a bitterly cold day in mid-January, it had snowed heavily overnight and the white fells seemed to crowd in even closer than usual above the little Cumbrian town of Bletchley Bridge.

Morning surgery at the Wilton Health Clinic had been brisk, in spite of the severity of the weather. Both Francesca Wilton and the senior partner Malcolm Westray had full surgeries, coping not only with their own patients but also those of their third partner, David Elcombe, who had just started a sabbatical.

'I'll be glad when this locum gets here,' said Malcolm irritably as he stomped into the staff-room at the end of surgery and grabbed a quick cup of coffee. 'When did you say he was arriving?'

'At the end of the week,' replied Francesca, 'or that's what David said before he left. He tried to get him to come earlier but apparently he's been abroad and has only just arrived in this country.'

'Well, the sooner he comes the better,' muttered Malcolm. 'We can't keep this pace up for much longer.' A giant of a man, dark and bearded, Malcolm Westray suffered from a duodenal ulcer and had been the least sympathetic to their partner's need for a sabbatical. He sighed as the intercom sounded. 'What is it, Ros?' he asked wearily.

'Emergency call from Sky Fell Farm,' the practice manager's voice came through. 'Sounds like Jeff Blake's having a heart attack.'

Francesca drained her mug then leaned across the desk to speak into the intercom. 'OK, Ros. Get his notes for me—I'm on my way. Is Jean Blake on the line?'

'Yes, she sounds pretty upset,' replied Ros. 'Do you want to speak to her first?'

'I shouldn't think there's much doubt with Jeff's history,' said Francesca, grabbing her case. 'I've warned him time and again to slow down and get some help with the farm but he won't listen.'

'I'll talk to her,' said Malcolm; 'you get going. Put Mrs Blake through to me, Ros.'

Leaving her partner to calm the distraught woman, Francesca hurried to her room and hastily donned boots and a waxed jacket, wound a woolly scarf round her neck and pulled a hat down over her unruly dark hair.

When she emerged a few minutes later Ros Price handed her Jeff Blake's medical records.

'I've sent for an ambulance,' Ros explained. 'Dr Westray told me to, after he'd spoken to Mrs Blake.'

'OK, Ros. Thanks. I hope the ambulance won't have trouble getting up there in this weather.' Francesca paused and looked out of the window. 'It's started snowing again,' she added.

'Would you like me to go?' asked Malcolm, coming into Reception behind her.

'Certainly not,' replied Francesca briskly. 'I'm on my way now.'

It had long been a bone of contention between herself and her partners that there should be no concessions towards her when it came to difficult calls regarding distance or weather conditions.

'Well, take it easy,' said Malcolm, frowning at the snow, 'no heroics.'

'As if. . .' Francesca pulled a face at him. 'But if it'll make you happier I'll take the Land Rover.' Flinging the end of her scarf over her shoulder, she picked up her case and tramped out of the building.

The snow in the car park had been churned into a slushy mess, making it decidedly slippery underfoot, and Francesca made her way carefully across to the practice Land Rover. Usually she preferred to drive her own, smaller car but in the circumstances it made sense to take the bigger four-wheel-drive vehicle.

The Blakes were sheep farmers and their farm up

at Sky Fell lived up to its name, situated as it was on the very crest of a narrow pass that wound its way over the fells. Jeff Blake had a history of heart disease and it had not surprised Francesca to hear he was in trouble again. She only hoped she would not be too late.

By the time she had driven out of the town it was snowing heavily, huge soft flakes like snowballs bursting against the windscreen in a relentless bombardment. The Land Rover held the road well but the going was slower than Francesca would have liked and she changed down to a lower gear to tackle the steep, slippery incline.

As she approached the road that ran along the top of the fells the weather degenerated into a full-scale blizzard. A cruel wind whipped the snow against the Land Rover, while by the side of the road twisted broom and gorse bushes, bent almost double with the constant battering of the elements, hid great banks of drifted snow that had fallen overnight. These same banks were now spilling across the road, creating an added hazard to driving.

At one point the windscreen wipers gave up under the accumulated weight of the snow, then, to Francesca's relief, manfully ground into action again. The vehicle's de-mister seemed to have packed up completely, however, and she was constantly forced to wipe the condensation from the inside of the windscreen.

Muttering to herself, she made a mental note to have words with Malcolm about the servicing of the Land Rover, which was his responsibility. As she wiped the screen for the umpteenth time a shape suddenly loomed up in front of the vehicle and Francesca jumped violently. Instinctively she braked to avoid whatever it was and the Land Rover slewed across the road. For one moment, through the driving blanket of snow, she mistook the shape for a sheep that had strayed on to the road.

Then as the shape moved she realised with a sense of shock that what she had thought to be a sheep was in fact a human figure, its dark coat encrusted with snow. Waving its arms, it approached the Land Rover.

Francesca wound the window down about two inches. 'You'll get yourself killed walking in the middle of the road like that,' she said sharply, and, not waiting for a reply, went on, 'What are you doing up here in this weather, for goodness' sake?'

'I'm trying to get to Bletchley Bridge but my car has broken down about a mile back.'

The voice was deep, male and cultured with a touch of authority about it. Francesca was surprised, as she had imagined it was a local man, maybe a lad from one of the farms.

'Bletchley Bridge is about four miles back.' She jerked her thumb over her shoulder, feeling a little foolish at having spoken so sharply. It was pretty obvious no one would be walking about in those conditions for the fun of it. But he had startled her, forced her to brake, could have caused an accident.

'Four miles!' There was a note of dismay in his voice.

Narrowing her eyes against the blizzard that was lashing through the gap at the top of the window, Francesca could just make out the outline of his features. Snow was sticking to his hair and eyebrows; his nose was pink. He looked frozen. She hesitated, then came to a rapid decision. 'I have a call to make at a farm about two miles further on,' she said, 'then I shall be going back to Bletchley Bridge. I'll give you a lift if you don't mind the wait.'

'Thanks a lot.' He shouted, but his voice was whipped away by the strength of the wind.

In the time it took for him to battle round the front of the vehicle, open the door and climb into the passenger-seat, Francesca had begun to have reservations about what she was doing. She wasn't in the habit of giving lifts, especially to strangers, and this man, by his lack of accent, clearly wasn't a local. Rapidly she came to a second decision and by the time he had slammed the door behind him she was talking to Ros on her mobile phone, telling her what she had done.

'I'll call in again from the Blakes',' she concluded.

'OK—I know what to do if you don't,' replied Ros.

By this time the man was wiping the snow from his face and hair. It was a lean face, she noticed, with finely chiselled features and a firm jaw, and the wing of hair which fell forward across the forehead was probably fair when it was dry. He was wearing a suede sheepskin coat and the snow which covered it was already beginning to thaw into little rivulets that trickled down on to the floor of the Land Rover.

'This is good of you,' he said, blowing into his cupped hands to warm them. 'I can't imagine you pick up strange men every day of the week.'

'You're right, I don't,' she said briefly, then as she let out the clutch she added, 'That's why I've let people know what I'm doing and where I am.' She glanced towards the mobile phone on the dashboard.

'Very wise.' He nodded. 'You can't be too careful these days. In fact in normal conditions I wouldn't even think of expecting a woman to give me a lift.'

'Yes, well, they're hardly normal conditions today,' Francesca replied crisply, peering through the windscreen at the even worsening blizzard.

They travelled in silence for a while then as they passed a car, apparently abandoned by the side of the road, only its outline visible beneath a mound of snow, she said, 'Is that yours?'

'Not exactly.'

'What do you mean?' She threw him a quick glance.

'It's a hired car.'

'So where were you coming from?' she asked a moment later, unable to contain her curiosity any longer in spite of her resolve not to get into unnecessary conversation with him.

'Penrith,' he replied.

'And you chose to come over the fells? In this weather?' Her voice took on a note of incredulity.

'It wasn't snowing when I left,' he replied ruefully.

They drove on in silence again then at last, to Francesca's relief, through the swirling whiteness she caught a glimpse of the roof and chimneys of Sky Fell Farm.

'Here we are,' she said, then half to herself she muttered, 'I only hope the ambulance will be able to get through.'

'Ambulance?'

She sensed the man's interested glance as she drove off the road and down into the farmyard. 'Yes,' she replied. 'The farmer's ill.'

'Are you a doctor?' he asked as Francesca opened the door of the Land Rover, leaning over the seat and picking up her case.

'Yes, I am.' Her reply was curt. 'Do you want to stay here or come inside?'

Before he had the chance to answer there came the sound of shouting from the farmhouse and Francesca jumped quickly to the ground. With her boots making deep indentations in the snow she battled her way through the still driving blizzard to the kitchen door.

'Oh, Dr Wilton—thank God!' A distraught Jean Blake met her in the doorway. 'It's happening again.'

'What's happening, Jean?' Francesca stamped the snow from her boots and followed her through the flagstoned kitchen where the heat from an Aga hit her cold cheeks.

'Pain, Doctor. He's in terrible pain,' gasped Jean. 'He was when I phoned, then I did exactly as Dr Westray told me and he seemed to get a bit better, but it's hit him again now.' As she spoke she led Francesca out of the kitchen and down a long narrow passage to the front of the house.

At the end of the passage Jean pushed open a door and Francesca followed her into a room which appeared to be some sort of office or study. A large desk beneath the window was strewn with books and papers and a pine log fire burned in the grate, its scent filling the air. Two black Labradors on the rug in front of the fire lifted their heads and thumped their tails on the floor. Jeff Blake was sprawled on an old leather sofa, a tartan rug covering his knees.

Francesca crossed swiftly to his side and knelt beside him, noticing as she did the bluish tinge around his lips and the clammy grey pallor of his face. Immediately she realised he had stopped breathing.

Glancing up at Jean, who hovered near the door, her hands covering her mouth in dread, she said, 'Help me get him on to the floor. Come on, Jean. . .that's right, flat on his back.'

Between them they managed to pull Jeff on to the floor and as Francesca searched in vain for a pulse she made sure there was no restrictive clothing around Jeff's neck. She was on the point of checking that his airways were clear when quite suddenly a voice behind her said, 'You breathe, I'll massage.'

She glanced up and saw that the man to whom she'd given a lift had followed her, not only into the house but also into the very room and was tugging off his sheepskin coat. Then, before she had the chance to even think, he was kneeling beside Jeff Blake on the faded red Axminster. There was something so positive about his manner that Francesca found herself accepting his offer. Hopefully he knew the rudiments of first aid and valuable time could be saved with two of them working over Jeff.

There was no time for further speculation as Francesca tilted Jeff's head back, pinched his nostrils and began breathing into his lungs while the man linked his hands together and began cardiac massage in hard rhythmic thumps just below Jeff's sternum.

It fleetingly occured to Francesca as they worked that the man had quite obviously done cardiac massage before; then she forgot the thought in the desperate struggle to revive Jeff.

For a time it seemed as if their efforts were to be in vain; they changed places twice and the man showed he was equally well-versed in the required breathing technique. Then, as Jean Blake sobbed uncontrollably in one corner of the room and all seemed lost, Jeff suddenly gave a choking gasp and began to breathe.

Francesca and the man stopped working and looked

at each other. Francesca nodded and the man smiled. His eyes were grey, she noticed irrelevantly, and his brows straight and dark.

'I think he'll do,' he said softly.

As Jean Blake realised what was happening she lowered her hands from her face and stared at them as if hardly daring to hope. Then as Jeff suddenly began groaning her shoulders sagged in sudden relief and the tears began streaming afresh down her face. 'Oh, thank you, thank you,' she whispered over and over again.

Francesca sat back on her heels and the man reached back in anticipation and, lifting her medical case from the floor beside the sofa, handed it to her.

'Thanks.' She sprung the catches and took a morphine ampoule and a syringe from inside. 'I'll give him an injection to ease the pain,' she explained to Jean.

'Do you have oxygen in the Land Rover?' asked the man as he got to his feet.

Francesca shook her head. 'No, but the ambulance will. Hopefully they won't be too long now.' She glanced at her watch as one of the Labradors suddenly nuzzled her hand.

'He's grateful too—you've saved his master's life,' observed the man with a faint smile. The smile transformed his face, giving warmth to the rather aloof expression that had been there before.

'He should be thanking you as well, in that case,' replied Francesca. 'You were a great help,' she added. When he merely shrugged in response, she said, 'I take it I can assume you've done this sort of thing before?'

'Yes.' He raised one eyebrow. 'Just a few times.'

Jean looked up then from the floor, where she was kneeling beside her husband. 'Well, thank you both,' she said, looking from one to the other. 'I dread to think what would have happened if you hadn't got here in time. . . Thank you, Dr Wilton and thank you. . .' She turned her head again to look up at the man, trailed off, then looked uncertainly at Francesca.

'I'm sorry,' Francesca also looked at him, 'I'm afraid I don't even know your name. . .' She glanced back at Jean and shrugged. 'I rescued this man from the blizzard; his car had broken down,' she explained.

'Oh, I see,' said Jean in surprise. 'I thought he was a colleague.'

'The name's Sinclair,' replied the man. 'And I would say one good turn deserves another.'

Sinclair? Francesca frowned. She'd heard that name somewhere quite recently, but she couldn't recall where.

The door opened and a teenage boy stuck his head round. 'Mum?' he said, his expression fearful as his gaze flew to his father. 'The ambulance is here.'

'Good.' Francesca scrambled to her feet. 'I'll go and speak to the crew. Will you go to the hospital, Jean?'

'Yes.' Jean nodded. 'My son has rung our neighbour at Dykefell, and he and his wife are on their way over—they'll come with me. I'll just go and get my coat and boots.'

The next ten minutes were busy; Francesca telephoned the coronary care unit at the local hospital to give details of Jeff's condition, rang Ros to say what was happening, then supervised Jeff Blake's transferral to the ambulance that was waiting in the yard. While Jeff was being given the oxygen he needed to help with his breathing, the Blakes' neighbours arrived.

When the ambulance drew away, followed by the neighbours' Range Rover, Francesca and her passenger climbed back into their own vehicle.

It had stopped snowing but the sky was still leaden and overcast as they drove out of the farmyard and turned on to the top road.

In the strange, yellowish, almost eerie light there was a hushed stillness as if the surrounding countryside held its breath, bracing itself for the next onslaught.

They travelled in silence, slowly, following the tyre marks in the snow of the two vehicles that had gone before them. It was not until they began the steep descent into the town that Francesca, without taking her eyes from the blinding whiteness of the torturous road, asked, 'Where to, in Bletchley Bridge?'

He didn't answer immediately and suddenly, unreasonably impatient, she added, 'Where would you like me to drop you off—the local garage? Although I doubt they'll be able to send anyone for your car today.'

'No.' His reply, when it came, was even, considered. 'Not the garage. I think the Wilton Health Clinic first.'

'The health clinic. . .?' She threw him a quick, startled glance but he was staring ahead and didn't answer.

Why would he want to go to the clinic? He wasn't a local so could hardly be a patient. So who was he? She frowned. He'd said he'd come from Penrith and that he'd been driving a hired car.

'Are you a medical rep?' she asked.

He laughed. 'Hardly. All self-respecting reps will be tucked away in their hotels in this weather.'

'What did you say your name was?' She struggled to remember.

'Sinclair,' he said, glancing out of his window as he spoke. 'Guy Sinclair.'

Sinclair. That was it. But where had she heard the name before? When he'd said it to Jean Blake it had rung a bell, but still Francesca couldn't think where she'd heard it.

She frowned and blinked, the brightness of the snow beginning to affect her eyes.

Guy Sinclair? Where had she heard that name?

She threw him another glance but he was still gazing out of the window, only his profile visible to her, that sweep of fair hair, the high-bridged, finely shaped nose and the firm line of the jaw.

Realisation, when it came, was quite sudden as the pieces fell into place in her mind, and immediately Francesca could have kicked herself for being so stupid.

She drew a deep breath. 'You're the locum,' she said flatly.

'None other,' he replied, half turning his head.

'We weren't expecting you until the end of the week.'

'I arrived in the country earlier than I thought.'

'So why didn't you say who you were?' she demanded. Suddenly she felt angry. Angry that he had in some way seemed to trick her.

'I didn't really have the chance,' he replied patiently, 'not after I'd discovered who you were—and let's face it,' he raised one eyebrow, 'there wasn't really time, was there?'

'No,' she paused, 'I suppose not,' she conceded finally, 'but I feel foolish now.'

'There's no reason to,' he replied easily. 'It just seemed the natural thing to do—to help.'

They fell silent again but when at last they drove into the town Francesca still felt annoyed that she hadn't known who he was. Not that logically she could have known; they weren't, as she had pointed out, expecting the locum until later in the week and she knew very little about him anyway—had only heard his name the once—but surely, surely later she should have known, when he had helped with resuscitating Jeff?

Because then, even if she had still failed to recognise him from the professionalism of his approach, then he should have told her.

In fact, the more she thought about it, the more convinced she became that he should have told her the moment she offered him a lift.

Damn it! After all, he'd known she was wary of taking a stranger aboard.

With a squeal of tyres Francesca skidded to a halt on the health clinic car park.

She switched off the engine and for a moment neither of them spoke.

'You'd better come in and meet Malcolm Westray,' she said tightly at last. 'I take it you don't know him?'

He shook his head. 'No; David Elcombe made all the arrangements.' As he spoke he opened the door, climbed out of the vehicle and walked round to her side. 'I take it he's left for New Zealand now?' he said, opening the door for her.

Francesca nodded and, ignoring his proffered hand, jumped from the Land Rover, only to slip on the snow. To her embarrassment she felt his hand beneath her elbow, steadying her. For a brief moment she leaned against him.

'Thanks.' She grimaced and, regaining her balance, led the way into the clinic, past the row of patients already assembling for the next surgery and up to the reception desk.

Ros, who was behind the desk, looked up as Francesca approached.

'Hello,' she said. 'Everything all right. . .?' She trailed off as she caught sight of Francesca's companion.

Francesca nodded. 'Jeff Blake is on his way to hospital,' she said, then, aware that Ros was still staring at the newcomer with barely concealed interest, she said, 'Is Malcolm in?'

'No, he's gone to fetch the kids from school,' Ros paused. 'Sarah's got a flat battery,' she added by way of explanation.

'I see,' Francesca turned and caught an amused smile on her companion's lips. 'The trials of domesticity,' she said lightly, then immediately wished she hadn't felt compelled to defend her partner's actions. 'Are you a family man?' She raised her eyebrows.

'No.' He grinned, bringing a glint to the steady grey eyes. 'I've managed to escape that condition.'

'Quite.' She turned back to Ros, who was by now staring in unashamed curiosity. 'Ros,' she said steadily, 'this is Dr Sinclair, our locum. Dr Sinclair,' she half turned towards him, 'this is Ros Price, our practice manager.'

'Oh!' Ros, clearly astonished, stepped forward and took his outstretched hand. 'Pleased to meet you, Dr S-S-Sinclair. . .' she stammered.

'Oh, please—Guy,' he said, shaking her hand then

glancing at Francesca as, including her, he said, 'Dr Sinclair sounds so formal.'

'We weren't expecting you yet. . .' mumbled Ros in confusion.

'So I gather.' Again that maddening raising of one eyebrow as he glanced back at Francesca.

'Oh!' Ros gazed from one to the other. 'Was it you who Dr Wilton picked up?'

'You could say that,' he replied drily.

'You'd better come through to the staff-room,' said Francesca abruptly, ignoring both his expression and Ros's apparent amazement.

She led the way into the staff-room, shutting the door firmly behind them.

'I would imagine,' she said coolly, 'you could do with some coffee?' Pulling off her hat and shaking out her dark hair, she crossed the room to the ever-bubbling coffee-pot.

'Thanks.' He nodded, watching her as she poured coffee into two mugs.

'Milk and sugar?' she asked without looking up.

'No,' he replied, 'just black, as it comes.'

'I understand,' she said as she handed him his coffee, 'that you will be using David's house while you are here?'

'Yes.' He paused, 'Is it far from the surgery?'

'No,' she replied. 'A stone's throw, that's all. I'm sure you'll be comfortable there, Dr Sinclair.'

'Please—Guy. Like I said to Ros.'

'Yes. Fine.' She drew in her breath. 'Although,' she added crisply, 'the staff don't call us by our Christian names in front of the patients.'

'Is that a fact?' He looked genuinely surprised. 'Where I come from we're a lot less formal than that. In fact,' he chuckled, 'most of the patients called us by our Christian names.'

'Really?' Coolly she looked at him, irritated by his ability to make her suddenly feel old-fashioned and stuffy. 'And just where is it you come from?'

'Well,' setting down his mug, he slipped off his

sheepskin coat and draped it over the back of a chair, apparently unperturbed by the coolness of her manner, 'Buckinghamshire originally, but I've recently spent some time in the States.'

'Ah, well.' She shrugged and, curling her hands round her mug, sipped her coffee, drawing comfort from the warmth.

He frowned. 'You said that as if my having been in the States explained something.'

She shrugged again. 'I understand they have a less formal way of doing things, that's all.'

'Maybe, but less formal needn't mean less caring.'

She felt herself flush at something in his tone. 'I wasn't suggesting otherwise——' she began, but he cut her short.

'Good,' he said smoothly. 'We need to get off on the right foot if we're going to be working together.'

'My sentiments exactly, Dr Sinclair,' she retorted.

'Guy.'

She hesitated. 'All right. Guy.'

'And your name? Surely you don't want me to call you Dr Wilton?'

'Of course not. It's Francesca.'

'What a beautiful name.'

To her dismay she felt herself flush again. 'It was my father's choice,' she said quickly. 'It was his grandmother's name—she was Italian.'

'That accounts for your dark Latin looks,' he said softly.

In sudden desperation she found herself searching for something to say in order to cover her confusion. 'My father founded this clinic,' she said hastily.

'And now?'

'Now?' She frowned. Suddenly she was very aware of him, so aware that she wished he would go—then she could finish her coffee and get on with her surgery.

'Yes, where is your father now?'

'Oh, I see. He's retired. He and my mother live in Scotland. He moved away so as not to meddle here, as he put it.' She found herself smiling in spite of herself as she recalled her father's retirement speech.

'So are you senior partner here?' Guy Sinclair, apparently in no hurry, perched himself comfortably on the edge of the table.

'No,' she replied patiently, 'that's Malcolm, Malcolm Westray—he's been here for years—then it's David...then me——' she broke off as the door opened. 'Ah, here's Malcolm now,' she said as the large figure of the senior partner filled the doorway.

Malcolm Westray stopped and looked from Francesca to Guy Sinclair then questioningly back to Francesca.

'Malcolm,' said Francesca, relieved at the interuption, 'you'll be pleased to know help has arrived sooner than you thought. This is Guy Sinclair. Guy——' she turned to the locum but as her eyes met his something in his expression caused her heart to skip a beat—'this is Malcolm Westray, our senior partner.'

The two men shook hands, then she took a deep breath and said, 'Now, if you'll excuse me, I'll leave you two to talk, as I have patients waiting for me.' Without so much as another glance in Guy Sinclair's direction but only too aware that his eyes were on her, she put her head down and made her escape from the room.

CHAPTER TWO

FRANCESCA tried to stay angry with him, or at least indifferent, because she knew from that very first day that she was attracted to him and she wasn't sure it was what she wanted. But Guy Sinclair's presence at the Wilton Health Clinic was like a breath of fresh air and her anger and irritation were soon forgotten.

Malcolm Westray and the new locum hit it off straight away and even if they hadn't done Malcolm would have been grateful just to have some of his workload eased.

When it came to the rest of the staff, the locum, with his brooding good looks and slightly aloof, almost aristocratic air together with an undeniable charm, very soon had them eating out of his hand. And he slipped into the routine of surgeries, house calls and daily clinics as easily as if he'd been at the practice for years.

The patients, once they'd got over their initial suspicion of anyone new, quickly adapted, and even the inevitable few, doing no more than seeking a second opinion, went away happy with Guy's method of handling the situation.

He moved into David Elcombe's house at the top of the hill behind the health clinic, a large stone building with a slate roof that had once been two farm labourers' cottages.

'All this must be very different from what you've been used to in the States,' Francesca commented one evening towards the end of his first week as she passed the open door of his consulting-room.

'In what way?' He looked up from his desk, the steady grey eyes meeting hers.

'I would imagine it's all a far cry from big-city medicine.'

'It was hardly big-city stuff where I was!' He gave

a short laugh. 'More small-town America. You know, real movie stuff; white fences and back porches—it really was like that.'

'Did you enjoy it?' She was watching him closely and thought, just for one moment, that she detected a slight hesitation before he answered.

'To a point.' He paused, looked down at his desk and began packing some instruments into his medical case. 'But it's good to be home again.'

'You certainly seem to have settled in quickly here,' she said.

'Ah, nice people—it makes all the difference.' He smiled, his eyes meeting hers again. 'And, talking of nice people,' he went on, unaware of the effect his smile had just had on Francesca's insides, 'have we heard how Jeff Blake is?'

'Doing very well.' The casualness of her tone, she hoped, did nothing to betray the turmoil of her emotions—a turmoil that was presenting itself with alarming regularity whenever Guy Sinclair was around. 'He should be home by the end of the week. I think this last episode has frightened him, though. At long last he's talking of taking on a manager to help him run the farm.'

'That sounds sensible,' Guy replied. 'It can't be easy running a sheep farm when one suffers with heart trouble.'

'The main problem with Jeff Blake is his stubbornness,' said Francesca drily. 'He's even determined to enter the sponsored walk we're arranging for one of Malcolm's patients—mind you, that shouldn't do him any harm,' she added.

'Sponsored walk?' Guy raised his eyebrows and not for the first time Francesca noticed how dark they were in contrast to the fairness of his hair.

'You mean you haven't heard about it?' She smiled.

'No; tell me more.' He leaned across the desk, not taking his eyes from hers as she explained.

'It's to help raise money for a little girl called Lauren Richardson. She's five years old and she has acute lymphoblastic leukaemia. The money is to send her and her mother and brother on holiday to Disney World in Florida.'

'Disney World?' He smiled. 'I remember it well.'

'You've been there?'

'Yes,' he nodded, 'when I was in the States. The hospital where I worked had a children's hospice in the grounds. We used to take parties of children to Disney World.' He paused. 'Put my name down for a sponsor form.'

'I thought you'd say that.' Francesca smiled at him, only too aware that the growing attraction she felt for him was mutual. She glanced at her watch. 'Time for home, I think,' she said, 'it's been a long day.'

'So where is home exactly?' he asked softly. 'I know it's somewhere on the other side of Bletchley. . .?'

'It's down on the Windermere road,' she replied, 'one of those cottages in the terrace by the bridge.'

'I know where you mean,' he nodded, 'I visited a Mrs Walsh there yesterday. . .'

'My neighbour.'

'It's a small world.' He paused. 'Have you eaten yet?'

She shook her head, knowing what was coming, not really sure if it was what she wanted, but somehow knowing she would not refuse.

'Let me cook for you.'

It was not quite what she had expected, had thought maybe he would suggest the new Chinese restaurant that had just opened in Bletchley Bridge. She raised her eyebrows in surprise.

'Oh, I can cook,' he said softly.

'I don't doubt it,' she replied.

'So will you let me prove it?'

'I don't see why not.'

They left the clinic together, Francesca only too aware of the speculative glances from Ros and the receptionists, knowing she was being drawn headlong into something she didn't seem to have the power to resist.

Before Guy Sinclair had erupted into her life she had been certain romance and commitment were things she really didn't want. Now she wasn't quite sure of anything. Her last serious relationship, before she had returned to Bletchley Bridge, had been with a man called Neil Smythe, a registrar at the Sheffield hospital where she had been working and with whom she had believed herself to be in love. It had all gone terribly wrong when Francesca had assumed he had wanted marriage, and in fact it had turned out that he seemed unable to commit himself to a long-term relationship.

Since then she had fought shy of serious involvment, concentrating instead on her career and in helping to maintain the practice that had been so dear to her father's heart.

But all that had been before the arrival of Guy Sinclair.

He cooked supper for her that night in the kitchen of David Elcombe's house and it was to be the first of many such occasions with either one of them, or sometimes both, preparing and cooking the meal.

On the rare occasions when they were both off duty, when Malcolm Westray was on call at his house in Ambleside, they would dine out, driving perhaps to Kendal or Hawkshead to intimate little restaurants that were to become firm favourites with them both.

Sometimes they discussed work, their careers and their individual attitudes to medical ethics and politics; the future of the Health Service and issues such as fund holding in group practice.

'Will the Wilton practice go for fund holding?' Guy asked her one evening as they lingered over coffee in a hotel restaurant on the shores of Lake Windermere, watching the pleasure crafts moor for the night.

'Probably,' she replied. 'We've delayed making a final decision until David's return—but it seems as if it's to be the way of the future and we don't want to be left behind.'

'It's a busy practice,' he observed thoughtfully, stirring a second cup of coffee, 'far busier than I imagined it would be.'

'Ah, you thought you were in for an easy ride when you came here?'

'Something like that.' He smiled at her across the table. 'It just goes to show—these tranquil English settings are not quite what they seem.'

'If you think this is busy,' she replied darkly, 'you just wait until the real season and the tourist invasion. . .I warn you. . .you ain't seen nothin' yet. . .'

He laughed. 'Don't you have any extra help in the season?'

'We haven't done in the past. . .but just recently,' she paused, 'we have discussed the possibility of taking on another partner.'

'Really?' He raised his eyebrows in interest but was prevented from commenting further by the arrival of the waiter with their bill.

'So why did you choose America?' she asked him on another occasion.

'I'm not sure really.'

They were leaning on the parapet of the bridge opposite Francesca's cottage, watching the water that cascaded from high in the fells foaming down over rocks and boulders until it reached the softer bed of the river, where it flowed smooth and fast.

'I suppose,' he went on after a while, 'I just wanted a change from England. . . I'd been in touch with a colleague who'd worked in the States and I was attracted by what he told me.'

'You worked in a hospital there?'

'Yes, in orthopaedics.'

'Had you ever considered general practice?'

'Considered it, yes.' He paused, reflecting, 'I even did my GP training and spent a year or so with a practice in Hull,' he went on after a moment.

'But. . .?' She turned her head to look at him.

'But I never really thought it was for me. . .'

'Will you go back to the States?' She found herself holding her breath as she waited for his reply.

'I don't know,' he said at last. 'I thought perhaps I would at one time.' He turned as he spoke, leaning back against the stonework of the bridge. 'Now I'm not so sure—things change. . .'

He kissed her that night. Just before he left to return to David's house. In the tiny hallway of her cottage when she said goodnight he drew her gently into his arms and kissed her, his mouth both tender and exciting, hinting at the passion that smouldered beneath the surface.

It was inevitable really. They had both known it would happen, that it was only a matter of time.

And Francesca was happy. Happy to live for the present, not to question what had happened in the past, or to wonder what the future would bring, to simply enjoy being with Guy, working alongside him and allowing their friendship to grow.

In March, when Wordsworth's daffodils were in bloom beside Rydal Water, the Wilton practice held their sponsored walk for Malcolm Westray's patient, Lauren Richardson. It was a twenty-mile walk carefully routed over the fells and both Francesca and Guy were able to take part while Malcolm held the fort at the surgery.

Lauren was there at the start to see them off, seated in her wheelchair, her head snugly covered by a brightly coloured woolly hat, hiding the ravages of chemotherapy.

The residents of Bletchley Bridge and the adjoining villages had surpassed themselves with their sponsorship generosity and were out in force to cheer the walkers. The loudest cheer was reserved for Jeff Blake, who dropped a kiss on the top of Lauren's head before taking his place with the other walkers.

'We'll keep an eye on him,' said Francesca to an anxious Jean Blake, who had driven her husband to the health clinic in the farm's Land Rover.

'I know you will.' Jean seemed relieved to know

that both doctors would be accompanying her husband. 'He was determined to go.'

'There's no reason why he shouldn't,' replied Guy as he laced his walking boots. 'He's made a first-rate recovery, he's done some training and the exercise and fresh air will do him good.'

The air was indeed fresh and invigorating as the walkers climbed the steep pathway out of Bletchley Bridge, for a brisk breeze whipped down from the fells, rippling the surfaces of the lakes far below. Above them white clouds scudded across a pale washed sky, changing the appearance of the landscape minute by minute, darkening then lightening the distant hills as they obscured then revealed the sun.

Francesca walked with Guy, happy in his company and at peace in her beloved Lakeland countryside.

By the time they stopped for a rest above Tarn Hows the breeze had dropped, the clouds dispersed and the deep almost emerald-green of the water sparkled in the spring sunshine. In the distance the peaks of the fells beckoned and a waterfall as white as snow cascaded from a high, hidden crevice.

'This has to be my favourite place,' said Francesca, surveying the scene. She was sitting beside Guy on a smooth boulder among ferns whose fresh green stalks pierced the crispness of last year's bracken, their leaves tightly curled, poised to unfurl. 'To me it brings back everything that was good about my childhood.'

'In that case,' murmured Guy, putting his arm round her, drawing her close, 'maybe it should be here that I tell you that I've fallen in love with you.'

It didn't really come as a surprise but his words thrilled her just the same.

'I know,' he went on when she leaned her head on his shoulder in response, 'that it's sudden, that we haven't known each other for long, but I can't help it. It's just happened, it's the way I feel. You see——'

But she silenced him then, stopped his reasoning by putting one hand over his mouth. 'Don't,' she whispered, 'don't explain. There's no need, because I feel the same.'

He moved his head, kissing her hand, the palm first, then her fingers, then, moving her hand so that he could lean forward, he kissed her mouth.

'I think we're being watched,' he said after a while, raising his head and looking across the bracken towards the others, who were sitting a short distance away.

'I don't care,' said Francesca. 'They probably all guessed anyway.'

Everyone, including Jeff, completed the walk and joined Lauren and her family in the health clinic for sandwiches and tea. The little girl looked tired but was flushed with excitement and her eyes shone as everyone talked of the trip that would now soon be possible.

'You'll love it.' Guy crouched in front of her wheelchair. 'It's magic.'

'Have you been there?' Her eyes widened.

'I have.' Guy nodded.

'Did you see Mickey Mouse?' she whispered.

'Of course.' Then, putting one hand beside his mouth, he whispered, 'Actually, he's a friend of mine.'

By this time Lauren's eyes were like saucers, then as Guy sat on the floor and unlaced his boots to relieve his aching feet, he groaned, smiled up at her and said, 'Say hello from me, won't you? Tell him the doctor who took the children from Honeysuckle House to see him—he'll know.'

Lauren giggled. 'Children like me?' she said. 'Children who can't walk?'

'Just like you, sweetheart.' Guy watched as Lauren's mother wheeled her away.

'Honeysuckle House?' murmured Francesca.

'The children's hospice I was telling you about.' Guy, his eyes suddenly bright, were still on Lauren as he replied.

He asked her to marry him shortly after that. She'd already sensed he was going to ask and was relieved. She didn't want another intensive relationship that was going nowhere, like the one she'd had with Neil.

This time, for Francesca, it had to be all or nothing, for quite suddenly, so suddenly in fact that it had taken her by surprise, she craved commitment. She was thirty-two against Guy's thirty-four; she wanted children and knew that he did too, and she also knew she couldn't put that event off forever.

'I'd like at least three,' he said during dinner at the hotel in Windermere on the night they became engaged.

'You've let yourself be carried away by Malcolm's kids,' she teased him laughingly.

'They're smashing kids,' he protested, then, growing serious, added 'But what if I have? It's what life's all about.'

'I know,' she said softly, touched by his simple philosophy.

'Trouble is,' he went on thoughtfully, 'before we have kids I need to think about how I shall support them.' He swirled the contents of his glass, watching the red wine stain the sides.

Francesca remained silent. She longed to tell him of the plan that had been forming in her mind for the past few weeks but knew she had to wait until David Elcombe's return.

'I thought, probably, back to hospital work,' he said after a moment. 'Perhaps paediatrics,' he added, 'or maybe orthopaedics again.'

David Elcombe returned to Bletchley Bridge in August and it took only one practice meeting and a follow-up appointment with the practice accountants for them to decide to ask Guy to be a fourth partner.

'I'm touched and honoured,' he told them simply when they formally invited him to join them.

'Don't get too carried away,' said Malcolm drily, 'we'll work you like a Trojan, believe me.'

'I don't doubt I'll survive.'

'So when's the wedding to be?' asked David, looking from Francesca to Guy then back to Francesca.

'Next month—after the main summer rush,' she replied.

David sighed. 'I don't know,' he said, shaking his head, 'I spend years trying to persuade Fran that what she needs is to settle down, to get married, to have a family, and what does she say? Tells me that marriage is quite definitely not on her agenda...so I retreat, defeated, to lick my wounds. Then what happens? I turn my back for five minutes, you come along,' he nodded curtly across the table towards Guy, who was leaning back in his chair surveying his old friend in amusement, 'and before we know where we are—it's wedding bells...! He trailed off. 'What it is about you, Sinclair? You always did manage to get the girls, even at medical school. What do you have that the rest of us don't? No!' He held up his hand as Guy opened his mouth. 'Don't bother to answer that question!'

'Where will you live?' asked Malcolm, ever the practical one, choosing to ignore the good-natured bantering between his colleagues.

'At my cottage to start with,' replied Francesca. 'Later we'll look for something a big larger, but the cottage will be fine for a while.'

'What about a honeymoon?' asked Ros later, dreamily.

'That might be a bit difficult,' said Francesca. 'I don't see how we can both be away at the same time.'

'Wouldn't your father help out?' asked Ros. 'He always said he would in an emergency.'

'I know.' Francesca laughed. 'But I'm not sure a honeymoon constitutes an emergency.'

'But of course you must have a honeymoon, darling. Your father and I will be down for the wedding and we'll simply stay on afterwards until you get back.'

'But——'

'No buts; I absolutely insist. Your father needn't dash around doing house calls, he can help out with surgeries.'

'I see you've got it all worked out.'

'I've waited a long time for this, Francesca, and it's going to be done properly.'

'Yes, Mummy.'

'Have you chosen your dress yet?'

'Yes, it's twenties style, in champagne lace and wild silk.'

'Oh? Not white?'

'No, Mummy—nor bridesmaids.'

'No? Oh, well, never mind.'

Smiling, Francesca replaced the receiver and turned to Guy, who had just come into her consulting-room. Happily, naturally, she slipped into his arms and lifted her face for his kiss.

'I'm thinking,' he said after a while, 'of asking David to be my best man. Would you mind?'

'Why should I mind?'

'I just didn't want there to be any embarrassment, after David's comments the other day.'

'There was never really anything between David and me,' she said quietly, then after a brief pause she added, 'I think at one time he would have liked there to be, but it would never have worked...it's as simple as that.'

'Fair enough,' Guy replied.

'So if he's not embarrassed, as far as I'm concerned there's no problem.'

A week before the wedding Lauren Richardson left for Florida with her family. Her health had been giving some cause for concern and there had been several delays over booking the holiday. Even at the eleventh hour there was some doubt as to whether she would be fit to travel. As the taxi finally bore them away to the airport an audible sigh of relief rippled around Bletchley Bridge.

Three days later Francesca's parents arrived and booked into the hotel in Windermere where the reception was to be held.

'I approve of your choice,' her father told her as they strolled together in the grounds of the hotel late in the evening.

'Well, that's a relief.' She laughed and tucked her arm through his. 'I can't imagine what your reaction would have been if I'd introduced someone inappropriate as a partner in your beloved practice.'

'What about someone inappropriate as my son-in-law?'

'I rather suspect you'd have said that was up to me, but the practice is another matter.'

He laughed and squeezed her hand, then, growing serious again, he said, 'Your happiness is of the utmost importance to your mother and myself.'

'I know, Daddy. I know.'

'And you are happy, aren't you?' There was just a trace of anxiety in his tone. 'This is all very sudden, you know.'

'I know.' Francesca's reply was firm, unhesitating. 'But yes, I am happy. Very happy.'

'Good. I like the man. He has a good brain on him and there's breeding there.'

Francesca laughed. 'Is there? I hadn't noticed. I simply love him.'

'Ah, but what are the qualities that make you love him?'

'I don't know,' she said simply. 'I just do.'

The heather had deepened and the leaves on the sycamores outside the clinic were turning to gold when Francesca and Guy were married in the tiny stone church in Bletchley Bridge. Francesca knew her mother would have preferred one of the larger churches in Windermere or Kendal but she'd stuck to her guns.

'We live in Bletchley Bridge,' she said; 'the practice is here. These are our people. They would be disappointed and hurt if we crept off somewhere else.'

Her words were confirmed by the size of the crowd that turned out to watch her arrival at the church and to wish her well.

And if she'd had any lingering doubts they were dispelled when, as she walked up the aisle on her father's arm, Guy turned and saw her and smiled as their eyes met.

The service, brief and simple but solemnly binding, reminded them both of the commitment they were making to each other: for better for worse, for richer for poorer, in sickness and in health...till death us do part... Words said so many times, by so many people...

Then afterwards out into the autumn sunshine, to the congratulations of family, friends and patients, to the flash of cameras, the swirling of confetti and to the vintage Bentley that whisked them away to their favourite hotel overlooking Lake Windermere.

Francesca's only regret was that so few of Guy's family had been able to attend. His parents were both dead, his brother lived abroad and only his sister, her husband and an elderly uncle were there.

'I'm so pleased you are here for Guy,' she told his sister Lavinia later at the reception.

'I wouldn't have missed it for the world.' Lavinia, uncannily like Guy with the same fair hair, straight dark brows and level grey stare, coolly kissed her cheek. 'I was beginning to think no one would ever tie him down.' Her look implied an interest in summing up just what it was about Francesca that had brought about her brother's capture. Her remark was harmless, without malice, but it left Francesca wondering just how many others had attempted the same thing.

Guy had arranged for them to fly to Spain for their honeymoon, to a villa that belonged to a friend, but they decided to spend their wedding night at the hotel in Windermere.

When the last of their guests had gone Francesca stood at the open window watching a hunter's moon that sat on the horizon shedding its light over the lake, while in the bedroom behind her the hotel manager arrived with champagne in an ice bucket.

As the door closed behind the manager Guy slipped off his jacket, tossing it on to the bed as he unfastened his tie and the top button of his shirt. Then he crossed the room to join Francesca at the window.

'I love you, Dr Sinclair,' he murmured, slipping his arms around her and running his hands down over the silk of her dress moulding her hips.

Francesca felt his lips touch the nape of her neck just as his fingers found the zip fastening on her dress.

'I love you too,' she whispered back, stiffening at his touch and arching her back; then, turning, she melted into his arms. Winding her arms around his neck, she sank her fingers into his thick fair hair and as she felt his lips on hers the champagne silk dress floated to the floor, settling like a cloud around her ankles. The next moment Guy lifted her into his arms and carried her to the four-poster bed.

CHAPTER THREE

IT WAS hot, even hotter than usual for Spain in September, but their honeymoon had been perfect, quite perfect. It was nearly over now, only two more days before they flew home, but Francesca didn't want it to end, wanted it to go on forever.

She stole a glance at Guy sitting beside her in the driving seat of the small car they had hired. His dark brows were drawn together in a straight line as he stared ahead at the narrow mountain road they were travelling. There had been signs earlier warning of rockfalls and although they hadn't seen any Francesca knew the conditions required her husband's total concentration.

Her husband. With a sigh she wriggled down more comfortably in her seat and continued to gaze unashamedly at Guy's profile. If she was honest she was still finding it hard to believe that this man actually was her husband, that she, Francesca Wilton, career woman and dedicated GP, who had once doubted that marriage was for her, had allowed herself to be swept so thoroughly off her feet.

At one time if anyone had even suggested that she would marry a man she had only known for a few short months she would have dismissed the idea as ludicrous, but that was before she'd met Guy Sinclair, and since then Francesca was the first to admit, things just hadn't been the same.

As if he sensed her scrutiny he threw her a glance, briefly risked taking his eyes from the road, and finding her watching him, took one hand from the steering-wheel and placed it lightly on her thigh.

The gesture was both tender and possessive and with another sigh, this time of contentment, Francesca leaned her head back, lifting her face to the sun.

Through the open sunroof a mischievous breeze teased loose strands of her unruly dark hair from the blue and white bandanna she wore, curling them into a wild tangle.

On one side a sheer rock-face towered above them into an endless blue sky while on the other, far below, neat terraced vinyards, guarded by dark sentinel-like cypress trees, stretched across the valleys for as far as the eye could see.

When Guy had first suggested coming to Spain Francesca, mindful of tourist traps and lager louts, hadn't been sure it was what she wanted.

'Trust me,' Guy had said when she voiced her fears, and the moment she had set eyes on the villa high in the hills above Calpe she was captivated. With its pink washed walls beneath a coral tiled roof, cool archways and terraced gardens above orchards of almond trees, and with distant glimpses of a sparkling Mediterranean, it was little short of paradise.

'Your friend must be very rich,' she'd said on their first evening when they'd dined on the mosaic-tiled patio. But Guy had merely laughed and refilled her glass with champagne.

And now, clad in beige linen shorts and a white shirt tied into a single knot beneath her breasts, with the sun hot on her smooth, tanned legs and a smattering of freckles across her nose, Francesca made a mental note in future to always trust her husband's judgement.

It had been something of a miracle really that they had managed to get away together from the health clinic, but everyone, goaded by Ros, had rallied round to enable them to have this break. Dear Ros, who had never married herself but who was such an incurable romantic. Francesca smiled to herself as she recalled how the practice manager had totally reorganised the rotas and surgery times. And she was grateful, more than grateful, for she desperately needed this time alone with Guy. Time to get to know him, for there had been so little of that.

There had been time to love him, time for passion,

she reflected dreamily as the car climbed on up the mountain, but very little time to really get to know Guy the person, as opposed to Guy the lover, or even Guy the doctor. That there was a lot more to learn she didn't doubt—a man didn't reach thirty-four without some sort of past. Maybe she had been blinded by the intensity of her feelings for him, she thought, and she had to admit that those feelings were like nothing she had ever known before.

Their honeymoon had had a magical quality about it as Guy had shown her a side of Spain she had only read about, a side as far removed from the travel brochures and the tourist sun-spots as it was possible to imagine. A Spain of timeless history, of proud people, of deep-seated tradition and culture, of rugged mountains, deep cool valleys, a land of castles, fortresses and monasteries and devout religion.

And when Guy made love to her it was as if they entered some undreamed-of dimension. The nights at the villa in their cool, misty blue bedroom with its dark Spanish furniture and thyme-scented bed linen had surpassed her wildest expectations.

'Are you happy?' he shouted above the sound of the engine as the little car ground manfully up the mountain road.

'Ecstatically,' she called back.

'We'll stop at the first village on the other side and find somewhere to eat.'

'All right. . .' She trailed off and settled back further into her seat. They were approaching another bend, a sharp one that totally obscured their vision of the road ahead, and she wanted to allow him to concentrate.

As they rounded the bend Francesca's only impression was of heat; overpowering heat that danced and shimmered above the surface of the road. A split-second later she caught sight of the rocks that had cascaded from above and littered the way ahead.

Later, Francesca was to recall the scene in a series of slow-motion flashbacks: the sun glinting on the windscreen of a red car travelling down the mountain towards them, her own soundless scream and Guy's warning shout as he braked and swerved to avoid the oncoming car.

She would recall lifting her arms to protect her face before the sickening, bone-jarring impact and the crunching of metal as their car hit the rocks.

Then came the silence. A terrible, awesome silence as if the mountains and valleys held their breath, waiting to see what devastation had been done.

Later, it would all seem different. But for the moment she had to find out if she was still alive, if this silence was, in fact, heaven.

Slowly she lowered her arms, lifting her head then cringing back again as nature, not to be outdone, retaliated. The low rumbling sound was followed by the thudding of yet more rocks, loosened by the impact, thundering on to the roof of the car and showering them with loose grit and particles of earth through the sunroof.

When all was still and silent again she lifted her head, even more cautiously this time.

Far below in the valley a single bell began to toll.

Wildly Francesca looked around. Guy was slumped forward over the steering-wheel, his face turned away from her. Instinctively she reached out and touched his shoulder.

'Guy.' Her voice was barely more than a hoarse whisper. To her dismay there was no response. 'Guy!' Desperately she fumbled with the clasp of her seatbelt and eventually managed to release it. Still Guy hadn't moved and, leaning sideways, Francesca reached out, her fingers automatically searching for a pulse. To her relief she detected the faint but steady throb at the side of his neck. 'Guy,' she repeated, more urgently this time, 'are you all right?'

He remained still and silent and Francesca felt the first stirrings of panic. Frantically she tried to release the catch to Guy's seatbelt but was prevented from doing so by the awkwardness of the angle. She was still struggling when she heard a knock on her window.

She turned her head sharply to find a man peering into the car. In a daze she stared back at him, and then he tugged open the door. He was a young man, little more than a teenager, his eyes hidden behind mirrored sunglasses.

Speaking in rapid Spanish, he began pointing at Guy, gesticulating excitedly.

Francesca scrambled out of the car, vaguely aware that she was all in one piece. At the same time she was conscious of a dull ache at the back of her neck and a sharper pain in her left shoulder, both of which she ignored in her desperate anxiety for Guy.

With the young man at her heels, still spilling his torrent of Spanish, she groped her way round to the driver's side, only to find that the front of the car and best part of the wing had caved in, the metal crumpled concertina-fashion. Scrabbling over the rocks that obstructed access to the driver's door, she began sobbing and tearing at them with her bare hands, trying to pull them away.

'I can't get to the door!' she gasped, peering frantically into the interior of the car. She could see Guy's face now, pressed against the metal doorframe. His eyes were closed and a trickle of blood ran from under his hairline and down the the side of his cheek. The position of his neck looked strangely twisted and for one dreadful moment Francesca feared his spine may be damaged.

She continued pulling the rocks away but soon realised that the metal of the door was so badly crushed that it would be impossible to open it.

The young man must have summed up the situation at the same instant, for he darted back to the passenger side and leaned across the seat to release Guy's seatbelt.

As it dawned on Francesca that he meant to pull Guy across the passenger-seat and out of the car she stumbled back and caught his arm.

'No!' she shouted. 'Don't move him!'

He turned his head and looked at her over his shoulder, his face ridiculously expressionless behind the mirrored glasses.

'Don't move him!' she repeated, searching in her memory but discovering that every word of Spanish she had ever known was forgotten in the trauma of the moment. Then, sensing the young Spaniard's bewilderment and afraid he was going to pay no heed, she said, 'I'm a doctor. A doctor.'

'Doctor?' He stopped and frowned, then eased himself out of the car again and straightened up. 'Doctor?' he said again.

Francesca nodded, breathing deeply then, looking frantically round and catching sight of his car, which had skidded to a halt a little further down the mountain, she said, 'Go and telephone.' As she said it she frantically mimed the action, afraid he wouldn't understand what she meant.

His frown cleared. 'Ah. *Sì!*' he said, then to Francesca's relief he turned and ran back to his car. She expected him to get into the car, to drive away, hopefully to summon help. Instead, he leaned inside, then emerged a moment later clutching a mobile car phone.

'Oh, thank God!' Francesca muttered weakly and leaned against the bonnet of the crashed car. The metal struck hot through the thin fabric of her blouse and as she moved smartly away the man ran back to her, waving the phone above his head in triumph.

'Ambulance,' she gasped and even to herself her voice sounded like a sob.

'*Sì*. Ambulance.' He nodded emphatically, then, crouching down by the side of the car, he pulled up the aerial of the phone and began punching out numbers. Seconds later he was talking again in his rapid Spanish, wildly waving his free hand as he did so.

Mindful of the fact that the car might catch fire but choosing to ignore the possibility, Francesca slid back into the passenger-seat and sat beside Guy. He was still unconscious but she felt helpless because she didn't want to move him until she had some sort of support for his neck. She had no idea how long it would take for the emergency services to arrive and as she sat beside Guy, gently stroking the arm that rested on the steering-wheel, she found herself praying that they would be in time.

Dear God, she couldn't lose him now. Not when she'd just found him, when she'd just learnt what it meant to really love someone.

The sun grew even hotter as it climbed higher in the sky and to Francesca the waiting seemed like an eternity. The young man sat by the side of the road, his head in his hands.

Then, at last, from far below at the foot of the mountain came the faint but unmistakable wailing of a police siren.

The young man lifted his head at the sound, then as it grew closer he stood up, waving his arms.

Moments later in a cloud of dust and to the squeal of tyres the rescue services arrived and before Francesca had time to even think the car was surrounded by uniformed police and paramedics.

As she struggled to explain what had happened, fortunately one of the paramedics seemed to be understanding her.

'I want a brace for his neck,' she said, barring all access to Guy by sitting firmly in the passenger-seat.

The paramedic nodded and ran back to the ambulance, returning almost immediately with a neck brace. Under Francesca's supervision the brace was fitted, then after a certain amount of careful manoeuvring the rescue crew extricated Guy from the twisted wreckage of the car and were able to lift him into the waiting ambulance.

Francesca was about to climb into the back of the vehicle when a sudden wave of giddiness and nausea swept over her. She might have stumbled but one of the policemen put a steadying hand beneath her elbow to assist her.

In the moment before the door closed, as she sat on a low seat beside Guy, she caught a glimpse of the young Spaniard as he began an excitable version to the police of what had happened.

The ambulance began its descent of the mountain and Francesca took Guy's hand, desperately trying to fight her despair as her mind raced ahead with the awful possibilities of what might have happened to him.

He was still unconscious, his face ashen in spite of the tan he had acquired, and she knew only X-rays would tell whether or not there was any sinister significance to the awkward angle of his head and neck immediately following the crash.

When the ambulance eventually stopped Francesca was vaguely aware of a large white modern building, then of acres of glass and tubular steel, of Guy being taken straight to the casualty department, of noise, excitable Spanish voices, white uniforms, questions she didn't understand, of trying to tell them that she was a doctor, that Guy was a doctor, that he could have damaged his spine, that her own shoulder was hurting. . . Then, as someone ushered her into some sort of treatment-room, of another wave of dizziness, of rising nausea, then of darkness enfolding her, closing in. . .of slipping to the floor. . .of startled cries. . . followed at last by peace and blessed oblivion.

Bright jewelled colours were shining on the white ceiling, forming patterns like those of a child's kaleidoscope.

'What is it, Mummy?'

'The sunlight on the diamond in my engagement ring.'

'I think we've captured a rainbow.'

And the rainbow was back, now on the ceiling above her. Francesca turned her head half expecting to see her mother. But the talk of rainbows had been when Francesca was a child in Cumbria.

She wasn't a child now and she wasn't in Cumbria.

But where was she? She turned her head again. She was lying on a bed in a white, airy room. Bright sunlight filtered through the slats of a venetian blind that covered the window.

She looked down and saw that it was a ring on her own finger that was catching the light, creating the rainbow on the ceiling.

Her ring, not her mother's.

Her engagement ring, the ring Guy had placed on her finger that night at the hotel in Windermere.

Guy. Suddenly she remembered and struggled to sit up. A pain shot through her shoulder and she cried out.

'Steady on.' The voice, coming from behind her, was calm, quiet and, mercifully, very English.

Francesca moved her head, more cautiously this time, and saw a woman of about her own age. She was small and fair with large, expressive brown eyes.

'Hello—glad you're back with us.' The woman was smiling. 'I'm Dr Ryder—Helen Ryder. You fainted back there—how are you feeling now?'

'All right—I think. . .' Slowly Francesca moved again, this time managing to sit right up.

'Well, take things steadily. . .'

'I have to get up. . . My husband. . .'

'Yes, I know.' Helen Ryder nodded reassuringly. 'Everything's under control. Your husband is in X-Ray at the moment. I've asked that they tell us as soon as there's a result.' She paused and stared shrewdly at Francesca, who made a supreme effort to pull herself together.

'My name,' she said at last, 'is Sinclair, Francesca Sinclair, and my husband is Guy. . .we are both doctors.'

'Yes, we know,' said Helen.

'I didn't think I'd been able to make anyone understand that.'

'José, one of our paramedics, is married to an English girl. He understood you.'

'And you're English. . .?'

The other woman nodded. 'Yes; I'm on a two-year contract here, but I like it so much I just might stay.' She grinned. 'It's the weather that's done it. I don't think I could cope with England again and all that rain.'

Francesca managed a weak smile.

Helen Ryder thrust her hands into the pockets of her white coat. 'Are you in general practice?'

'Yes,' Francesca nodded, 'in Cumbria.'

'Cumbria? How long have you been there?'

'I've been a partner for two years,' Francesca replied.

'And your husband? Is he a partner as well?'

'Almost. . .' Francesca paused and Helen Ryder raised her eyebrows. 'He's in the process of buying a partnership,' she explained then added, 'We've only just got married.'

'You mean. . .?'

'Yes.' Francesca sighed ruefully. 'We're on our honeymoon.'

'Oh, I say,' the other woman suddenly looked concerned, 'what a perfectly beastly thing to have happened—look, you stay put for a moment and I'll go and see what's happening with your husband.'

'Thanks.' Francesca watched her walk to the door, then said, 'It was his neck I was worried about—it seemed to be twisted at such an unnatural angle.'

'I know.' Helen Ryder nodded. 'But let's not speculate at this stage. I'll be right back.'

As the door closed Francesca lay back against the pillow and closed her eyes. What Helen Ryder had said was true; it really was a beastly thing to have happened. In fact, she still couldn't really believe it had happened. It had been so quick—one moment they had been enjoying the scenery, the sunshine and the sheer pleasure of just being together. . .and the next, there had been the rockfall in the road, the red car hurtling towards them on the wrong side of the road, then Guy braking, exclaiming, swerving, and the sickening impact as metal hit rock. . .

Then there had been that silence, a silence so awesome, so deafening that Francesca thought she would remember it until the day she died. And even the relief she had felt at finding that Guy was alive had been quickly overshadowed by the terrifying possibility of a severed spinal cord. . .

She sat up and leaned forward, running her fingers frantically through her hair. Dear God, don't let that have happened.

She knew the implications, had seen it all before—had worked with quadriplegics when she'd been doing her training, knew all their limitations. . .

Likewise she knew what could be achieved, what they could be capable of, even after the most disabling accidents. . .

But not Guy. . .a wave of panic washed over her. . . please not Guy. Guy, who was so full of life, who lived every minute as if it were his last. . .surely. . .

'You can relax.' Helen Ryder strode back into the room, breaking into her thoughts.

'You mean. . .?' Hardly daring to hope, Francesca stared at her.

'See for yourself.' Helen was carrying an X-ray folder, which she dumped unceremoniously on the bed.

Aware that her hands were shaking, Francesca drew out the plates and held them up to the light. Her experienced eye told her what she needed to know.

'You see, no sign of any fractures,' said Helen. 'Apart from a lump on his head and a few lacerations and grazes to his left leg, he was virtually uninjured. And you'll be pleased to know he has apparently just come round.'

'Oh, thank God!' Francesca murmured, lowering the plates. 'Can I see him?'

'Of course.' Helen gathered up the plates and put them back in the folder while Francesca swung her legs to the floor and stood up, wincing as a pain shot through her shoulder again.

'I think we should X-ray that shoulder before we let you go,' observed Helen.

'Oh, I think it's only a bump—just bruised, I expect.'

'Even so,' Helen shrugged, 'to be on the safe

side—can't have you going home with stories of inefficiency in Spanish hospitals.'

'OK,' Francesca managed a smile, 'if you insist. But I must see Guy first.'

'Come on—I'll take you to him.' Helen held the door open and stood back as Francesca walked cautiously across the room. To her relief there was no reoccurrence of the giddiness or nausea that had caused her to faint.

She followed Helen Ryder down a wide corridor, its floor tiled with brightly coloured mosaics, to a small private room not unlike the one she had just vacated; she crossed the threshold, her heart leaping with relief as she caught sight of Guy. He was sitting on a cane chair facing the large picture window and there was no sign now of the dreaded neck brace.

'Dr Sinclair,' Helen Ryder crossed the room and stood in front of him, 'I've brought someone to see you.'

Guy stared up at Helen and as Francesca watched him from the doorway her heart ached with thankfulness.

'Someone to see me?' His voice was hesitant, without its usual note of authority, but that was understandable, Francesca thought, in view of what he'd been through.

'Yes.' Helen inclined her head slightly towards Francesca. 'Your wife.'

Francesca had been about to move forward but something stopped her. Guy was still staring at Helen Ryder but his whole body had stiffened.

'My wife. . .?' he said slowly, incredulously. He half turned his head, so Francesca could see his profile, but still he didn't take his eyes from Helen's face. 'Chloe. . .?' he said and the bewilderment in his voice was only too obvious.

Francesca frowned, poised on the threshold, then as Guy finally turned his head towards her she caught her breath and stepped right into the room, anticipating his smile.

His face was comparatively uninjured with only a slight graze on his forehead just below his hairline. But as his gaze met hers not only was there was no smile, there was not even so much as a flicker of recognition, and the expression in his grey eyes remained totally blank.

Francesca felt the smile fade from her own lips and she glanced uncertainly at Helen, who was frowning at her.

'I'm sorry,' said Helen, 'I thought you said your name was Francesca.'

'It is,' said Francesca quietly, transferring her gaze back to her husband's blank stare. Taking a deep breath, she crossed the room and stood before Guy's chair. 'Hello, Guy,' she said softly. Bending forward, she lightly kissed his cheek. 'How are you feeling?'

'OK. . .I think.' He stared up at her. Still there was no trace of recognition in his eyes. If anything, what she saw there was suspicion.

Taking another deep breath and steeling herself against an awful possibility which was becoming more probable by the moment, Francesca crouched before him. 'Guy,' she said urgently, 'we've been in a car crash—do you remember?'

He shook his head.

She tried another tack. 'Guy, do you know where you are?'

Still he looked blank, then he glanced at Helen Ryder. 'Hospital?' he said.

'Yes.' Francesca nodded. 'Do you know where the hospital is?'

'The States?' he said. 'Virginia?'

'No.' She swallowed. 'Not the States, Guy. Spain. We are in Spain.'

'Spain!' The incredulous look was back on his face.

Leaning forward and trying to ignore the panic rising inside her, Francesca took his hands and gripped them tightly. There was no comforting responding grasp. 'Guy,' she tried again, her voice low, 'Guy, do you know who I am?'

He continued to stare at her.

Silently she gazed back, willing him to say her name. Then slowly he shook his head. 'No,' he said. 'I don't. Should I?' His tone was polite and he glanced up at Helen, who was forced to look away in sudden embarrassment.

In the end it was Helen who broke the silence in the room. 'I think,' she said, bending down and touching Francesca's arm, 'that we should leave your husband to rest for a while. Perhaps, Francesca, you'd like to come to my room?'

In a daze Francesca left Guy still sitting in his chair staring out of the window, and followed Helen Ryder down the corridor to her own consulting-room.

When Helen had closed the door behind them she turned to Francesca. 'It's probably only temporary,' she said bluntly. 'You know that as well as I do.'

'Yes, I know.' Francesca nodded, then inhaled deeply. 'It was a shock, that's all.'

'I can imagine,' Helen replied sympathetically.

'He didn't even know me,' muttered Francesca half to herself.

'Give him time. . .he had quite a bang on his head, you know.'

'But when you said his wife had come to see him he expected to see someone called Chloe.'

'Has he been married before. . .?' began Helen curiously.

'No,' said Francesca. 'No. . .at least. . .' She paused. 'No, of course not,' she said firmly.

'So do you know anyone called Chloe?' Helen frowned.

Francesca shook her head. 'No. I've never even heard him mention the name before.'

'Well, like I said,' Helen shrugged, 'I shouldn't worry too much—the mind can play funny tricks, and after all, he didn't even know he was in Spain, did he? Didn't he say he thought he was in the States?'

'Yes. . .'

'Do you know why he would have thought that?'

'He was living in the States before he came to Cumbria...' Francesca began.

'And when was that?'

'Almost eight months ago...'

'Have you only known him that long?' Helen raised her eyebrows in surprise, and when Francesca nodded she said, 'A whirlwind romance, then?'

'Yes, you could say that,' Francesca agreed then felt compelled to add, 'Although I'm not usually such an impulsive creature.'

'Can't say I blame you.' Helen grinned unexpectedly. 'He's a very attractive man.' She paused, then, growing serious again, she went on, 'But like I said, I shouldn't worry too much if I were you.' In an obvious attempt to be matter-of-fact, she added, 'You don't need me to tell you that amnesia can be quite common after a head injury and it's usually only temporary.'

'And what if, this time, it isn't?' Francesca ran her fingers through her hair in sudden desperation.

'Let's not speculate at this stage,' said Helen firmly. 'The first thing for you to do is to establish just how much he does remember. But you must take it slowly, Francesca; don't rush him. His memory may return suddenly, or gradually, over a period of time.' She stopped and began toying with a folder on her desk. 'At least he knows who he is,' she mused after a moment, then more positively she added, 'And he also knows he's a doctor—that's a very good indication that not too much has been lost.'

'But he doesn't know me!' said Francesca through gritted teeth. 'He looked at me as if he'd never set eyes on me before.'

'Give him time,' said Helen again. 'Now, what I suggest is that we take you down to get that shoulder X-rayed, then I think you could go back to where you are staying.'

'And Guy?' Francesca looked up sharply.

'I think I would like to keep him here overnight—just for observation,' Helen said. 'You can have him back in the morning. Are you happy with that?'

'It doesn't look as if I've got a lot of choice,' replied Francesca helplessly as Helen stood up and opened her office door.

CHAPTER FOUR

A FAINT morning mist lingered in the valley but the sun felt warm even at that early hour. Francesca took her breakfast on the patio just as she had done every morning since coming to Spain, but there the similarity ended, for on every other occasion Guy had been with her, seated across the table in his white towelling bathrobe, his hair still damp from his morning swim. This morning his chair was empty.

In two hours' time she would collect him from the hospital and bring him back to the villa. Looking down at her hands, she saw that her knuckles were white where she was gripping her mug of tea too tightly.

Abruptly she stood up.

She had to be positive. David Elcombe had indicated as much when she had put a call through to him the previous night.

'We've been involved in an accident, David.' Putting it into words had brought home the reality of the situation and she had begun to shake.

'Good God! What's happened?' David's voice, although full of concern, was instantly reassuring. 'Are you hurt?'

'No. No, I'm OK. Just a few bruises. . .'

'And Guy?'

'Well. . .I'm not sure. He was knocked unconscious; at first I thought he may have damaged his spine. . .'

'For goodness' sake! Did they——?'

'Oh, yes, his treatment has been first class and his X-rays were clear. . .'

'So what's wrong?'

'They're keeping him in hospital overnight for observation. . .'

'That's normal. You know that, Fran, especially following concussion.'

'I know, I know, David. . .' Her voice shook.

'Then what. . .?'

'He didn't know me.'

'Didn't know you?' He paused. 'You mean amnesia?'

'Apparently so.'

'Again, that happens. . .' His voice was soothing now. 'What degree are we talking about?'

'I don't think a very high degree—he knows who he is. . .and the fact that he is a doctor. . .'

'Well, that's something.' There was a decided note of relief in David's voice.

'But beyond that,' she went on quickly, 'I'm not really sure. I shall know more tomorrow when I pick him up.'

'Will you come home on the flight you planned?'

'Yes, provided Guy is fit enough to travel.'

'Is there anything I can do, Fran?'

'I don't think so, David. . . Oh, yes, just one thing. Will you tell Malcolm and the rest of the staff for me. . .warn them?'

'Of course. . .' David lapsed into a helpless silence as if unsure what else he could say, then more positively he added, 'I'll make sure there's someone to meet you at the airport. . .and Fran. . .?'

'Yes?'

'Don't worry. He'll be fine.' His voice was reassuring again. 'It'll only be a temporary thing, I'm sure.'

She recalled David's words later that morning when the taxi dropped her off in the hospital grounds. I only hope he's right, she thought as the cheery Spanish driver promised to return in half an hour. Because if he wasn't and Guy's amnesia proved to be permanent she could have major problems on her hands.

Helen Ryder, looking cool in a crisp white coat, her fair hair drawn back into a single plait, came to meet her in Reception then led the way into her office.

'How is he?' In spite of her own medical training Francesca was only too aware of the anxiety in her voice. It was so different being on the other side of the fence, seeking reassurance instead of giving it.

'Physically there's nothing wrong with him, apart from the bump on his head and the slight injuries to his leg,' replied Helen, scanning a report, presumably Guy's, on the desk before her.

'And mentally?' As Francesca spoke her gaze was on Helen's face and she was grateful that when the other woman glanced up she met her stare squarely.

'There are,' Helen replied firmly, 'still things he can't remember, but the essential things are all there, like his identity, his family background and his training.'

'And what about me?' Francesca's voice was low, anxious. 'Does he remember me now?'

'Apparently not.'

'So, aren't I essential?' Her voice almost stuck in her throat.

'Of course you are, Francesca.' Helen's tone had softened. 'But it seems as if it's the more recent past that has been obliterated. He can remember his childhood, his family—he knows his parents are dead and he spoke of a sister and a brother.'

'So what period of time are we talking about?' Francesca frowned.

'I'm not really sure.' Helen shook her head. 'I was hoping you could help there.'

'Me?' She raised her eyebrows. 'I don't see how if he can't even remember me.'

'He spoke of America. . .'

'Yes. I told you, he had been working out there.'

Helen was silent for a moment as if considering, then she said, 'Do you know how long he was there?'

'About a year, I think,' Francesca replied slowly. 'It may have been longer; I'm not absolutely sure.'

'Well, his long-term memory seems to cease shortly after his arrival in the States.'

'So he's lost somewhere between eighteen and

twenty months,' Francesca said quietly, then, standing up, she walked slowly to the window and, lifting one corner of the venetian blinds that were lowered against the glare of the sun, she stood looking out at the palm trees that fringed the hospital grounds. A small boy was playing with a brightly coloured ball on a patch of dry brown grass. Even as Francesca watched, the ball bounced across a pathway out of her vision, the boy ran to retrieve it and was followed by a young, dark-haired woman who, seconds later, led him firmly back on to the grass.

Helen remained silent, giving her time to come to terms with the facts.

Eventually Francesca dropped the edge of the blind and turned to face the English doctor. 'What can I do to help him?' she asked simply and the question was one between two women rather than between two doctors.

'Just keep everything as normal as possible,' Helen replied levelly, then, seeing Francesca's expression, she added, 'I know that may be easier said than done, but I believe it's the only approach to this type of condition.'

Francesca stared at her. 'So is that it?' she asked slowly at last. 'Is that all I can do?'

'There is no treatment, Francesca,' Helen replied patiently, 'but you don't need me to tell you that, just as you don't need me to tell you that there is every chance that his memory will be completely restored.' She paused, allowing Francesca time to digest what she was saying. 'But it could take time,' she went on after a moment, 'and it may not all come back at once. He may just recall snatches at first, glimpses of his recent life as one would view a scene by lifting a curtain then letting it drop again.' She nodded towards the Venetian blind to illustrate the point she was making. 'You will need to be very patient, very understanding. It may not be easy, Francesca, especially at first. . .'

'He's my husband,' Francesca's voice wavered slightly, 'and I love him.'

'Exactly.' Helen smiled. 'And that's why you'll succeed. You'll be just fine. I know you will.' She paused, 'You'll keep in touch?'

'Of course.' Francesca's frown cleared. 'I am so grateful for all you've done, Helen, and for your kindness. And if you do decide to come back to England, please pay us a visit.'

Helen Ryder stood up and laughed. 'I may just take you up on that. The Lake District is one of those places I've always meant to visit but never got around to.'

'Who knows,' Francesca smiled, 'you may end up staying...like Guy has...' She trailed off uncertainly, suddenly overwhelmed by thoughts of home, the practice and the problems she had to face in the next few days.

'And when you do return,' replied Helen firmly, ignoring her apparent apprehension, 'that beautiful scenery I've heard so much about could well be the trigger required to restore his memory.'

Francesca nodded, knowing Helen could well be right, but at the same time wondering why *she* couldn't have been the trigger. She was his wife, for heaven's sake...and he'd looked at her as if she was a stranger...thought she was someone called Chloe... whoever Chloe was...

'Right, so if you're ready we'll go and find your husband.' Helen's voice broke into her thoughts, then she walked round her desk, opened the door and stood back for Francesca to precede her out of the office.

For one moment Francesca hesitated, afraid of what was to come, then, squaring her shoulders, she took a deep breath. She had to be positive, not only for Guy but also for her own sanity. After all, there was a very good chance with every passing hour that things could rapidly return to normal and they could pick up their lives where they'd left them before that fateful moment on the mountain.

When she walked into the room where Guy had spent the night she found him ready and waiting for her. He was wearing the same cream polo shirt and khaki shorts that he'd been wearing at the time of the accident, and although his tan seemed to have paled a little and his features looked rather drawn he looked exactly the same.

Apprehensively she stepped forward, then relief seemed to flow through her veins as the merest suggestion of a smile touched his lips. Suddenly, she longed to take him in her arms, to hold him, but even as she took another step towards him he lowered his gaze as if he found it impossible to maintain eye contact with her. And in that instant she knew that the apparent recognition in that smile had only been from seeing her the previous day and nothing else.

Helen walked to the taxi with them and after they had installed Guy in the rear seat she stood for a moment beside Francesca in the hospital car park. The sun was hot on their shoulders while all around them the bustle and sounds were of a normal morning at the busy hospital. To Francesca it felt unreal, as if it were happening to someone else, as if she were viewing the events and not actually taking part.

'Just give him time,' Helen murmured taking Francesca's hand and squeezing it tightly. Then she stood back as Francesca got into the taxi beside Guy.

The last glimpse she had of Helen was as the taxi drew away and as she glanced back through the rear window she saw the doctor raise her hand in farewell. A wave of desolation swept over Francesca and suddenly she felt very much alone, which was ridiculous really, especially as she had just got her husband back.

She stole a glance at him but his face was turned away from her, his profile set, inscrutable, as he gazed at the narrow streets of the old Spanish town. Maybe, she thought hopefully, the return to the villa might just stir something in his memory. . .the villa where they had been so happy. . .where they had made such passionate love.

She watched him after that, as unobtrusively as possible so that he wouldn't be aware of it, but, at the same time, closely, in case he showed even the slightest glimmer of remembering his surroundings.

They took the wide dual carriageway out of the town and as they left the high, closely packed buildings behind their route took them through vineyards, orange and almond groves, into open countryside then through more orange groves as the road began to climb steeply to the colony of luxurious villas that dotted the hills high above the town of Calpe.

Far below them the vast expanse of the Mediterranean glittered in the morning sun merging on the distant horizon with the equally startling blue of the sky.

Still Guy remained silent but by the time the taxi swept through the black wrought-iron gates of the villa and crunched to a halt on the loose gravel of the drive Francesca had convinced herself that he knew where he was.

While she paid the driver Guy climbed stiffly from the car and stood looking around him, then as the taxi disappeared down the drive she turned eagerly to him.

'Do you remember staying here, Guy?' she asked breathlessly.

Slowly he nodded, and her heart leapt.

'Yes, I do,' he said hesitantly at last, then, frowning and at the same time dashing her hopes, he added, 'but it was a long time ago.'

He stood for a while looking up at the villa, the pink washed walls, the shaped coral tiles on the roof and the ornamental wrought-iron grilles covering the arched windows.

'This is John's place,' he said slowly at last as if it had been a great effort remembering, 'John Travers,' he added, his expression clearing. 'He's a merchant banker,' he explained without looking at her, 'my father and his were great friends. . .' He turned and looked back across the valley. 'I used to spend holidays here when I was at school.' He said it wonderingly as if he was surprised that he should find himself there again. Not waiting for Francesca to comment, he strolled across the terrace, and, for all the world as if he were an ordinary holidaymaker just arrived at his destination and checking out the facilities, he leaned over the small stone parapet and stared into the blue depths of the swimming-pool.

'You don't recall coming here since?' Francesca tried to keep calm, to keep the anxiety from her voice.

He turned then and looked at her. 'No.' He shook his head slightly. 'Should I?'

'We've been staying here for the past ten days,' she replied quietly.

He continued to stare at her and she wondered what he was thinking.

'We've been on holiday?'

The question was totally innocent and in the circumstances wholly appropriate, but Francesca felt her hands curl into tight fists by her side.

'We are on our honeymoon,' she said quietly, watching helplessly as she saw the bewilderment come into his eyes.

'I didn't realise. . .' His voice was suddenly husky and he trailed off, uncertainly turning his head away from her again and staring out over the valley once more.

She longed to touch him, to help him in his bewilderment but something stopped her, something held her back, some instinct warning her that too much too soon could cause irreparable damage.

'Helen. . .' She gulped. 'Dr Ryder didn't tell you?' she asked.

Guy shook his head again. 'No, she said. . .she said you were my wife. . .but I thought. . .I don't know what I thought. . .' He shrugged helplessly. 'I suppose I imagined we'd been married for some time. . .' He stared at her again, a frown creasing his forehead. 'When. . .?' he said at last. 'Where?'

She flinched at the blankness in his eyes, hurt, in

spite of her resolve not to be, that all recollection of their wedding-day had gone.

Stepping forward, she joined him at the parapet, resting her arms on the cool stonework and watching the bright sunlight dancing on the water.

Taking a deep breath, she said, 'We were married ten days ago in England.'

He had turned his head to look at her but at her words he straightened up and stepped back from the parapet, a look of utter amazement on his face.

'What the hell was I doing in England?' he said slowly. 'I thought I was in America.'

'You were.' A breeze rippled through her dark hair, blowing tendrils across her face. 'But you came to England afterwards,' she explained, 'to do locum for a friend.'

'What friend?' He still looked totally bewildered and Francesca knew with sudden certainty things were going to be much more difficult than she had even feared.

'David Elcombe,' she replied patiently. 'Do you remember him?'

'David Elcombe?' he said slowly. The same breeze had tousled his hair, the colour of which reminded Francesca of ripe wheat, blowing it across his forehead, giving him a boyish, vulnerable look.

'Yes,' he went on after a moment, 'I do remember him; we were at medical school together, but I haven't seen him for. . .' he shrugged again '. . .for years.' He paused. 'Have I?' he asked suspiciously when Francesca remained silent.

She swallowed. 'Yes, Guy,' she said, 'you have. David is one of my partners.'

He continued to stare at her as if she was talking rubbish then with an exasperated sigh he ran one hand through his hair, pushing it back from his forehead.

'Oh, God, I'm sorry,' he said and there was a rough, raw edge to his tone, 'this must be a nightmare for you. . .'

It was the first time he had acknowledged the existence of her feelings but instead of making her pleased his anguish only fuelled Francesca's longing to help him.

'If only I could remember,' he muttered through clenched teeth, turning away, then as if something had just occurred to him he swung round and said sharply, 'You said David Elcombe is your partner?'

'Yes.' Francesca nodded. 'I'm a GP.'

'I knew you were a doctor,' he said slowly. 'Helen Ryder told me.'

'What else did she tell you?' Francesca was watching him closely.

'Not very much.' The frown between his brows had deepened. 'She said she didn't want to confuse me, that you would fill in the details.' He paused and briefly closed his eyes as if struggling to clear the mists in his brain. 'So where do you practise?' he asked at last, opening his eyes again.

'I'm a partner in a practice in a place called Bletchley Bridge; it's in the Lake District,' replied Francesca. 'Does that ring any bells?'

He shook his head.

'I just wondered if it might. You see, you are in the process of buying a partnership in the same practice.'

Silence followed her words, a silence in which Guy simply gazed at her in astonishment.

'Did I hear right?' he said at last. 'Did you really say I was buying a partnership?'

'I did,' she replied quietly.

'Me?' His tone was incredulous now. 'In general practice?'

'Is that so terrible?'

He gave a helpless shrug. 'No, I suppose not. Not really. It's just that I thought I had made up my mind to stick with orthopaedics. I never thought I would go into general practice. . .so why now? I can't understand it.'

'Don't you think marrying me might have had something to do with it?' Francesca asked quietly.

He continued to stare at her and for a fleeting

moment she thought she detected panic in his eyes. Was he summing her up? Wondering why on earth he'd married her? What the hell he'd seen in her?

In an effort to fight her own rising panic she turned away, sick at heart at what had happened but still uncertain how she should be handling it.

Keep everything as normal as possible, Helen Ryder had said.

It was worth a try. Taking another deep breath, she said, 'I'll get us some iced lemon tea, we've been drinking that each morning about this time instead of coffee. It's far too hot for coffee, and you like lemon tea.'

'Yes,' he agreed, 'I do like lemon tea.' There was a note of surprise in his tone as if he was pleased he had remembered. The fact, simple as it was, somehow heartened Francesca too and with a brief smile she hurried into the villa.

Maybe it wouldn't be too long before everything clicked back into place, she thought as she took ice cubes from the fridge and put them into two tall glasses. And even if they did have this problem for the time being, it really was good to have Guy back and to know that he didn't have any serious physical injury.

They spent the rest of the day quietly at the villa, swimming in the pool and resting on sun loungers. At Francesca's suggestion Guy refrained from asking more questions, spending the time simply trying to relax and resting after his trauma.

Later, in the cool shade of the fig tree in the corner of the patio, Guy fell asleep and Francesca found herself watching him, loving every line of his lean muscular body, longing for him to open his eyes, to turn to her and begin to caress her, to make love to her as he usually did.

Maybe, just maybe. . .this sleep would clear his mind. . .

An hour later his eyelids flickered and he opened his eyes.

Francesca held her breath.

Slowly he turned his head and looked at her and her heart missed a beat.

Then he frowned and glanced round him in bewilderment. For one dreadful moment she thought he had not only forgotten events of the past eighteen months but also of the last two days; then he pulled a hand across his face and sat up.

For a long time he sat on the side of the lounger, his back, bronzed from their days in the sun, towards her, his head in his hands.

Her heart went out to him.

Quietly, she sat up and swung her legs to the ground so that she too was sitting on the edge of her sunbed, then, unable to restrain herself a moment longer, she leaned forward, reached out and impulsively touched him.

As her fingers made contact with the smooth, bronzed skin he flinched, stiffened, lifting his head as an animal would when it scented danger, then in a purely involuntary movement he drew sharply away from her.

Francesca recoiled, withdrawing her hand as swiftly as if it had been burnt, and stood up, so abruptly that the movement upturned her sunbed.

Guy, startled, looked round and in that instant must have realised what he had done from the wounded look in her eyes.

'I'm sorry,' he muttered, staring at her, then, turning his head away, said again, 'I'm sorry.'

'It's all right.' The moment was over and she replied quickly, too quickly in her attempt to disguise the hurt she inevitably felt at his rejection.

'Oh, God,' he groaned, 'this is awful.' He covered his face with his hands again. 'I wish I could remember.' His voice, although muffled, could not hide his despair.

'You will,' she whispered, 'I'm sure you will—it may be gradual, but in time, you will.'

'And if I don't?'

She had moved round by then to stand in front of

him and he lowered his hands and looked up at her.

'You don't need me to tell you,' he said brutally, 'that amnesia sufferers don't always regain total recall.'

She stared back at him helplessly for a moment, then, trying to keep the despair from her voice, she said, 'Well, if that's going to be the case then we'll just have to rebuild our lives as best we can.'

'What do you suggest? Counselling? Therapy sessions?' There was undisguised sarcasm in his voice now.

'If that's what it takes, yes!' she said. 'There's nothing wrong with counselling or therapy; they've helped a lot of other people, and there's no reason why they shouldn't help us. Being doctors doesn't make us immune to life's problems, for heavens sake!'

He didn't reply, simply raised one eybrow in the way she had once found endearing but which now, to her sudden horror, infuriated her.

'It could have been worse, Guy,' she went on after a moment when he remained silent, 'it could have been much, much worse—you could have forgotten everything; who you are, your family background, your medical training, everything. As it is, you've only lost about eighteen months. The last eighteen months.'

'A very crucial eighteen months by the sounds of it,' he replied wryly. 'Not only do I find I've returned from the States and apparently got married, but it sounds as if I've also changed the course of my career——'

'I still say it could have been so much worse,' she broke in. 'Why, at the time of the accident I was afraid you'd broken your neck!'

He'd turned his face away but at her words he looked up sharply.

'Honestly, Guy,' she said passionatcly, 'it was that bad! I feared the worst. This is bad, damn it! But you must stop feeling sorry for yourself! Losing a bit of your memory is nothing compared to the prospect of spending the rest of your life in a wheelchair. . .' She choked and trailed off, horrified not only at what she had just said, but also to find that hot, angry tears were trickling down her cheeks.

With a helpless little gesture she lowered her head and, ignoring Guy's sudden exclamation, she hurried into the villa.

CHAPTER FIVE

IN THE kitchen Francesca angrily brushed away her tears with the back of her hand then pressed her burning face against the coolness of the fridge.

Why in heaven's name had she said those things? The last thing she had meant to do was upset Guy, and now it looked as if she'd done just that. And if that wasn't enough, her shoulder had started to ache, nagging away like a persistent toothache. If anyone had asked her, she would never have believed it possible for life to change so drastically in such a short space of time.

'What's the matter with your shoulder?'

Sharply she lifted her head and saw that Guy had followed her into the villa and was standing in the open doorway watching her.

'Nothing,' she mumbled, moving away from the fridge.

'Yes, there is,' he said quietly, 'you were rubbing it and you looked as if you were in pain.'

'It's nothing really. I just bruised it in the crash, that's all.'

He stared at her for a long moment, then said, 'You must be thinking what an unfeeling brute I am.'

'Why?' She looked at him quickly, 'Why should I think that?'

'Well, I've been whingeing on about my loss of memory and I haven't even asked if you were hurt.'

'I didn't think. . .'

'It's true and I'm sorry.' Helplessly he spread his hands.

'It's OK,' she whispered, the tears dangerously close again. She wasn't sure she could cope with his sympathy.

'Let me see that shoulder.' To her dismay he crossed

the kitchen and moved round behind her. She braced herself, not because of the pain she might feel from the bruised shoulder but against the familiar feel of his hands on her bare flesh. As his fingers gently probed and examined she felt her muscles tense.

'Did you have this X-rayed?' he asked after a moment.

'Yes, it was OK,' she replied breathlessly. 'In fact, Helen let me see the X-ray for myself.' As she spoke she turned her head. His face was very close to her own, so close that she felt his breath on her cheek. In normal circumstances an episode like this would have ended with laughter, with her in Guy's arms, with him undressing her, carrying her to the bedroom or even making love to her on the spot. It had been a game to them to make love in every room in the villa—only the kitchen remained—but Guy didn't know that now, didn't remember their game. . .didn't even remember her.

'Try and relax,' he said. 'You're very tense.'

'Yes, I know. . .'

'Did you have any other injuries?' He was obviously remembering how to be a doctor if not a husband.

'Not really; my back was a bit sore after the impact but it's all right now.'

'Good. The bruising on that shoulder will fade in time.' He paused and moved away from her, then as she began preparing their meal he leaned on one of the worktops, watching her.

His silence was just beginning to make her feel uncomfortable, especially as she was trying to recover from the sudden nearness and his touch, when unexpectedly he said, 'Tell me about the crash.'

'What do you want to know?'

'Well, for a start, where did it happen?'

'In the mountains, above Calpe,' she replied carefully, then added, 'We were in a hired car——'

'Was I driving?' he interrupted.

'Yes.' She paused, at the same time lifting salad from a vegetable rack on to the worktop. 'We were about halfway up the mountain and we had just rounded a sharp bend.' She threw him a quick glance to see if her words had struck any chord in his memory. 'There was a rockfall,' she continued when he remained silent, 'It had blocked one side of the road.'

'A rockfall?' He frowned.

'Yes.' Bending down, she took a bottle of white wine from a wooden rack on the floor. 'There had been notices warning of rockfalls.'

'So what happened? Did I hit the rocks?' He looked incredulous.

'Yes, but it wasn't that straightforward.' She opened the fridge door and put the wine inside to chill. 'There was another car, travelling towards us down the mountain. It came round the bend very fast and swerved to avoid the landslide.'

'Good God! So did I hit him?' Straightening up from the lounging position he had adopted, Guy stared at her.

'No,' she said quickly, 'you swerved to avoid him, but in doing so you hit the rocks. Mind you,' she added when she saw his horrified expression, 'it was a jolly good job you did—there was a sheer drop on the other side. If you'd hit the other car we would probably both have gone over.'

He continued to stare at her as if trying to take in what she had just told him. 'And the other driver?' he asked at last and the inevitable note of dread in his voice was unmistakable.

Francesca shook her head. 'He was fine.'

'Wasn't he injured?' He sounded amazed.

'No. He didn't hit anything. He stopped his car a little further on then came back to us. . .in fact it was him who called the emergency services on his car phone.'

'His car. . .' Guy mused slowly and something in his tone made Francesca look up. She had chopped the cucumber and a red pepper and had just started on a large yellow pepper, but she stopped, her knife poised.

'What about his car?' she said.

'I don't know...I'm not sure.' He hesitated. 'Was it red?'

She stared at him, the knife still in the air. In the silence that followed the only sound to be heard was the endless singing of the cicadas in the trees around the villa. 'Yes,' she replied at last, 'it was.'

He stared back at her, then in a gesture of helplessness raked his fingers through his hair.

'Do you remember it, Guy?' she asked urgently. 'Do you remember the car?'

'I don't know...I'm not sure...'

'But you knew it was red?' she persisted.

'Yes, yes, I knew it was red,' he admitted. 'At least,' he paused, 'I think I did.'

'It was a Fiat,' deliberately she set the knife down, 'a red Fiat, and the driver was Spanish, a young man, no more than twenty or so—he was wearing jeans, I think,' she went on eagerly, 'yes, jeans and a dark green shirt...'

Guy stared at her for a long moment then shook his head. 'It's no good,' he said. 'I don't remember anything else.'

'No, of course you wouldn't remember the man, you were knocked unconscious in the crash...but the car...you would have seen that...you've remembered it was red. It's a start,' said Francesca emphatically. 'Helen said it might happen this way.' She picked up the knife again and began slicing the pepper. 'Just glimpses to start with,' she added with what she hoped sounded like encouragement.

'I'm not even sure it was that,' Guy replied tightly. 'It was probably just a calculated guess. After all, there are a lot of red cars about.'

'In Britain maybe,' retorted Francesca quickly, hopefully, 'but there aren't so many in Spain. I've noticed that; most of the cars seem to be white or grey, light colours...' She trailed off as she realised Guy was shaking his head.

'Clutching at straws,' he muttered, 'that's all we're doing.'

'And what if we are? It can't do any harm,' she declared stubbornly.

'Won't do a lot of good either.' He gave a short, derisive laugh then, catching sight of her expression, he sighed. 'I'm sorry,' he said, 'none of this can be easy for you. . .'

She shrugged. 'I still think that glimpse might have been a start, and I'm going to go on believing that.' Gathering up all the salad, she placed it in a large wooden bowl. 'Tomorrow,' she went on after a moment, 'we fly home, and any one of a hundred things might jog your memory. But for the moment, why don't we just concentrate on the present and enjoy our last evening in this lovely villa?'

'Sounds like a good idea to me.' He shrugged then smiled. It was his old smile, the one guaranteed to turn her knees to jelly.

They ate dinner on the terrace in the cool of the evening, an evening soft with the fragrance of jasmine, beneath a wide, star-studded Spanish sky, an evening made for romance, an evening perfect for lovers. Their talk was of Spain as Francesca told Guy of the places they had visited, some he remembered from his previous visits to the country while others were a blank in his memory.

As the sky deepened to indigo and a pale crescent moon appeared over the sea they lingered over their coffee and Francesca wondered what would happen next. When she had shown Guy into their bedroom on his return from the hospital he hadn't said a word. He'd stared at the double bed that they'd shared for the past ten nights, but he hadn't said a word.

Even as she wondered, he stood up and for a moment remained very still, staring down at her.

'I think I'll go to bed,' he said at last. 'It's been a long day.'

'Yes.' Francesca swallowed. 'I'll just tidy up.'

He appeared to hesitate. Should she suggest sleeping in another room? Maybe to avoid embarrassment that would be the kindest thing. But Helen had said to keep everything as normal as possible and, after all, Guy was her husband.

She remained silent and after a moment he turned and walked slowly into the villa.

Francesca remained where she was, allowing her thoughts to wander. She longed for Guy to make love to her, especially as it was the last night of their honeymoon, but at the same time, reluctantly, she was forced to admit that the chance of that happening seemed pretty remote.

Eventually she realised a chill had crept into the air. She stood up, sighed, then began clearing the table, carrying the dishes into the kitchen.

There was no sound from the bedroom and when at last after taking a shower she quietly pushed open the door it was to find Guy in bed lying on his side, his face turned to the wall.

Soundlessly she undressed, slipped on the cream satin nightdress she had chosen with such care for her honeymoon, smoothed it down over her hips, then carefully eased herself into bed beside her husband.

For a long time she lay in the darkness staring up at the ceiling. She knew Guy was awake but he didn't move or speak. She longed to reach out and touch him but dreaded the same reaction she'd had earlier on the terrace. She felt she could just about accept the fact that he didn't remember her, but she knew she couldn't cope with his rejection.

And the one thing she still had to face, the thing she hadn't dared to mention for fear of what she might learn, was the identity of the mysterious Chloe.

There was no getting away from the fact that when Helen had told Guy his wife had come to see him he had thought she was someone called Chloe. Even though she had never heard him mention anyone by that name she knew the issue would have to be faced. . .

But not yet. . . Helen also had advised that.

Maybe later, when he got his memory back.

If he got his memory back. . .

After a long time Guy's breathing deepened and Francesca knew he was asleep.

Hot tears slid from beneath her eyelids and ran unheeded down her cheeks. Then at last, feeling as if her heart was breaking, she turned on to her side, away from Guy, and attempted to sleep.

David Elcombe was at the airport to meet them. Dear, safe, familiar, David with his stocky figure and crisply dark receding hair. Casually dressed in navy polo jumper and cords, he was waiting for them as they came through Customs.

'Fran!' He stepped forward and kissed her cheek, then turned to Guy. 'Guy. . .?'

'Hello, David.'

The two men shook hands and to her horror Francesca felt the tears prick her eyelids. Then in her struggle to get her emotions under control she found herself watching Guy's reaction to meeting David. In reality it was less than a couple of weeks since they had last seen each other, but as far as Guy was concerned he hadn't set eyes on David Elcombe for a number of years. Neither man commented, however, on the bizarre nature of the situation and Guy helped David to stow their luggage in the boot of his BMW.

'How are things at the surgery?' asked Francesca a little later as they joined the traffic on the motorway. She was sitting beside David, as Guy had elected to sit in the rear seat of the car.

'Very busy.' David pulled a face. 'We'll be glad to have you two back, I can tell you,' he added, speaking half over his shoulder to include Guy.

'And how has my father been coping?' asked Francesca, thankful that David was treating the situation normally.

'Oh, he's been in his element,' David replied with a short laugh. 'Couldn't resist ruling the roost again, of course. . .we sent him packing back to Scotland a couple of days ago so that he and your mother can go off on their holiday—otherwise he would have been taking over.'

They both laughed, then David said, 'No, seriously he's been marvellous—don't know what we would have done without him. Our workload seems to have increased so much just lately. Best thing we could have done taking you on, Guy,' he called over his shoulder.

Guy remained silent but Francesca shot David a grateful glance; grateful for implying there was to be no problem over Guy's partnership and grateful that he had supposedly not informed her parents of what had happened. The last thing she wanted would be for them to cancel their annual holiday in Ireland, which they would have been sure to do if they'd heard of the accident and its consequences.

David continued to chat easily for the remainder of the journey and by the time they reached Bletchley Bridge some of Francesca's apprehensions at meeting the rest of the staff had disappeared.

'I expect you'll be wanting to get home,' said David as he swept into the car park of the health centre, 'but I thought it best to come here first to pick up your car.' Francesca guessed that what he really meant was that it would be a good thing to get the first meeting with the rest of the staff over and done with.

They walked into Reception and when Ros and the other girls greeted them so normally Francesca found herself wondering whether David had in fact told them what had happened.

But before she had time to speculate any further Malcolm strolled out of his room and peered at them both over the half-glasses he wore for reading. 'Hello, you two,' he said, 'good honeymoon?'

'Wonderful thanks, Malcolm—nearly decided to stay,' Francesca smiled and turned to Guy, 'didn't we, darling?' Guy nodded and managed a faint smile but she could see the signs of strain on his face together with a wariness in his eyes and, glancing round at the others, she quickly added, 'If no one minds, I think we'll get on home now and sort ourselves out.'

There were murmurings and noddings from the others and as David walked them to the door again he said, 'I'll talk to you later, Fran.'

'Yes, of course, David, thanks,' she said gratefully. 'And thank you for coming to the airport; I really appreciate it.'

'It was the least I could do.' He helped them transfer their luggage from the boot of his car to hers then watched as they got into the car, raising his hand as they drove out of the car park.

'Well, that wasn't too bad, was it?' Francesca said as she swung the car into the road.

Guy didn't reply and she shot him a swift glance. He was staring straight ahead, his expression dark, brooding.

'Guy. . .?'

'Yes?' He answered without looking at her.

'I said, that wasn't—'

'I know,' he cut her short, 'I heard you.'

'Well?' She frowned.

'It was horrendous.'

Her hands tightened on the steering-wheel. 'I'm sorry, I thought it went rather well under the circumstances.'

'Don't patronise me,' he said tightly.

She flushed and bit her lip. 'I wasn't patronising you, Guy. I genuinely thought it went well.'

'Do they know. . .about me?' he demanded.

'Yes, I spoke to David on the phone. I thought it better they should know. . .'

'That just makes it worse.' He scowled and glared sullenly out of the window.

'But I thought it went so well,' she protested. 'Everyone acted so normally. In fact the whole thing went much better than I dared hope it would.'

'Why? What were you expecting would happen?' he asked brutally. 'Did you think your friends would stare and poke fun at me as if I were some sort of freak in a sideshow?'

'Of course not,' she cried, shocked by his attitude.

'I knew they wouldn't do that. . .and they're not just my friends, Guy. They are yours as well.'

'Really?' he said coolly. 'So what was it you were afraid these friends might do?'

'Nothing. I simply thought that first meeting might somehow be embarrassing or difficult for you, that's all. . .' She lapsed into miserable silence.

'I'm sorry,' he muttered a few minutes later. 'But you can't imagine what it's like. . .having people greet you, talk to you, knowing everything about you. . . when you haven't a clue who they are.'

'Oh, Guy,' she threw him a helpless glance, 'I'm sorry too. Maybe we handled that all wrong. Maybe we should not have acted as if nothing had happened. I just don't know. . . We shall have to talk things through in future so that I know exactly what you want to do.'

In silence she drove out of Bletchley Bridge, through the avenue of horse chesnut and sycamore trees which while they had been away had taken on deeper tints of autumn. After crossing the little stone bridge she brought the car to a halt in front of the terrace of cottages where she lived.

She glanced at Guy to see if there was any recognition on his face but he was sitting very still, apparently waiting for her to explain why they had stopped.

'This is home,' she said quietly. 'At least, for the time being it is.'

'Oh?' There was a note of apprehension in the single word.

'Yes; we will be looking for something a bit bigger very soon. This cottage was fine for one but it'll be a bit cramped with two of us.' She opened the car door.

'You mean it was your home before I came?' he asked.

'Yes.' She glanced over her shoulder and saw that he was frowning. 'It seemed the most sensible thing that you should move in with me.'

They carried the luggage up the path between them and Francesca had just put her key in the door when a window in the adjoining cottage was opened and her neighbour Alice Walsh looked out.

'Welcome home!' she called, waving to them.

'Thank you, Alice,' Francesca replied. 'How are you? How's the leg?'

'Much better, thanks,' Alice replied. 'Did you have a nice time in Spain?'

'Marvellous.' Francesca smiled and nudged Guy.

'Yes, wonderful,' he agreed, taking his cue from her and smiling at the woman. 'I take it I know her?' he said as they stepped into the tiny hall of the cottage and Francesca shut the door behind them.

'Yes,' she nodded, 'that's Alice—Mrs Walsh. You treated her for phlebitis recently.'

'You amaze me,' he replied drily, but this time there was no bitterness in his tone.

'So was I living here before, before we were married?' he said a moment later as he gazed round him; at the hall, the stairway that curved round out of sight and the open archway that offered a glimpse of the sitting-room with its oak-beamed ceiling, soft floral furnishings and the kitchen beyond.

'No,' Francesca replied. 'You were lodging at David's.'

'I thought we may have been living together.' He seemed vaguely surprised.

'No.' She shook her head. 'You lived at David's house while you were doing locum for him; it seemed sensible that you remained there until after the wedding. Besides, I'm a bit old-fashioned about things like that.' She paused. 'I couldn't have had us leaving for the church from the same house. . .it would have been unlucky. . .and my mother would have had a fit. . .' She trailed off, aware she was waffling and that he was staring at her in apparent amazement. 'Leave the cases,' she said abruptly, 'we'll see to them later. I'll put the kettle on. I expect you could do with a cup of tea as much as I could.' She hurried through to the kitchen and Guy started to prowl round as if to get his bearings.

'Where are my belongings?' he said a few moments later, appearing in the archway.

'Upstairs,' she said quietly. 'You brought them over just before we went away.'

He seemed to accept that and was content to wait until they'd had tea before investigating further. But then, while Francesca was unpacking, any hopes she might have had that the sight of his possessions might restore his memory were quickly dashed when he wandered into the bedroom with a framed photograph of his parents in his hands.

'The last time I saw this was in America,' he said. 'It was on my desk at the hospital.'

Francesca glanced up. 'Is being in America still your last recollection?' she asked.

'Yes,' he said abruptly, setting the photograph down on the pine dressing-table then sitting heavily down on the side of the bed. He was silent for a while as if reflecting, then slowly he said, 'I clearly remember arriving at my lodgings in the town—it was a small town, in West Virginia—near Charleston—and of taking up my position at the hospital.' He stopped.

'Go on,' said Francesca, suddenly acutely aware how little she knew about him and ashamed that she had never encouraged him to talk more about his past before they were married. But there had been so little time...they had been so caught up in the present, in each other, that the past had ceased to exist.

'I was involved in a research programme,' he said slowly. 'Had I told you that?'

She nodded. 'Yes, you said it was to do with finding alternatives to orthopaedic surgery.'

'That's right.' He looked suddenly pleased that they should both be discussing something that he actually remembered.

'Do you remember anything else about your time in the States?' she asked curiously, suddenly mindful again of the mysterious Chloe, whoever she was.

'Yes, I remember people...' he hesitated '...colleagues, and patients—places I visited...but,' he stopped again and shook his head, 'it's patchy, hazy, if you know what I mean, as if I'm viewing it all through a net curtain.'

'And you can't remember anything since?' she asked quietly, achingly, longing for him to look up, to recognise her, to remember all they had shared.

Slowly, as if he couldn't believe it himself, he shook his head. 'No,' he said, 'nothing.'

'Ah, well,' she began, 'we'll just have to give it time——'

'But where do we go from here?' he asked abruptly, cutting her short.

'What do you mean?' Troubled by his tone but knowing full well what he meant, Francesca found herself playing for time.

When she had first come into the bedroom she had opened the window in order to air the room after its being shut up for so long; now a slight breeze stirred the curtains and at the movement Guy looked up.

'I think,' he said harshly, 'it's time to stop any pretence.'

'There is no pretence, Guy——'

'You said I was in the process of buying into the partnership,' he said, ignoring her protest. 'Just how far have those negotiations gone?'

She stared at him, then gave a faint shrug. 'The solicitors were finalising things when we went away.'

'I would imagine,' he said brusquly, 'there's an opting-out clause that I can exercise.'

'No, Guy,' she said sharply as she realised what he was saying, 'there's no need for that.'

'Isn't there?' He raised his eyebrows. 'I wonder if your partners would agree?'

'I'm sure they will. . .'

'Are you?' He gave a short, derisive laugh. 'I wouldn't be so sure. What possible use could I be to them in this state?'

'But you haven't forgotten how to be a doctor, for heaven's sake!' she cried. 'You've only forgotten——'

'How to be a husband?' he interrupted quietly.

'No!' she cried passionately, aware his gaze had flickered to the bed. 'No, Guy, I didn't mean that.'

He shrugged and turned away. 'I'm not sure how I'm supposed to be a good husband when I don't even remember meeting you, let alone marrying you,' he said bluntly. 'And as for being a GP, do you honestly think your partners are going to risk their reputations, to say nothing of their patients' welfare, by taking a chance on me?'

When she didn't reply, he went on, 'Come on, think about it. I could have forgotten all sorts of crucial factors to do with diagnosis or treatment.'

'But you haven't. I'm sure you haven't,' Francesca protested. 'You've lost about eighteen months of memory at the most.'

'Try telling them that,' he replied grimly. When Francesca remained silent, he went on, 'And to be fair to them, if it was the other way round I would be wary. I probably wouldn't take a chance on me either.'

'Let me talk to them. . .' she said desperately.

'By all means,' he shrugged and stood up, 'but I guarantee it won't change anything.' He walked to the door.

'Where are you going?'

'For a walk. I need some air. Oh, don't worry,' he said bitterly as her expression changed, 'I'll remember my way back.' He clattered down the stairs and out of the front door and Francesca sat down miserably on the bed. His frustration had become like some tangible thing between them and her heart ached with foreboding, not only for Guy but for herself and for their future.

She sat still for a long time then at last got up, closed the bedroom window, picked up the telephone receiver and dialled the surgery number.

'Ros,' she said when the practice manager answered, 'it's me, Francesca. Is Malcolm or David still there?'

'Yes,' Ros replied, 'they are both here. Who would you like?' she asked and Francesca was certain she could hear the sympathy in the other woman's voice.

She swallowed. 'Either will do.'

A moment later she heard Malcolm's voice at the other end of the line.

'Francesca,' he said, 'what can I do for you?'

'We need to talk, Malcolm,' she said, coming straight to the point.

'Yes,' he agreed, 'we do. But you must be tired. . . perhaps tomorrow.'

'No, Malcolm. Tonight. I need to talk tonight,' she replied.

'Very well. Would you like me to come to you?'

'No,' she said quickly, 'no, not here. I need to see you and David alone, without Guy.'

'Yes, I understand,' he replied. 'In that case, hold on one moment while I check with David. . .' He was back almost immediately. 'Yes,' he said, 'David is on call, so he suggested we meet at his house—say in half an hour?'

'Yes, Malcolm, that's fine.' She tried to keep the tremor from her voice but as she replaced the receiver her hands were trembling.

CHAPTER SIX

'ALL I'm asking is that you give him a chance,' said Francesca, looking at the two men across David's kitchen table.

'What do you say, Malcolm?' David glanced at his partner and Francesca bit her lip. If there was to be any difficulty she sensed it would come from Malcolm rather than David.

'It's worse than I thought.' Malcolm leaned back in his chair and pulled at his beard. 'I thought at first it was just memory lapse following concussion, but you say he's lost about eighteen months?'

'Yes,' Francesca nodded, 'but——'

'I foresee all sorts of problems.' Malcolm cut her short. 'And you're suggesting we keep it from the patients?'

Francesca nodded and glanced anxiously at David for support.

'I don't see their knowing would serve any purpose,' David said and Francesca breathed a sigh of relief. 'Guy hasn't forgotten how to be a doctor—he's merely lost a section of his recent memory. Unfortunately it's the section that includes meeting and marrying Fran.' David paused, then after a long moment during which no one spoke he went on, 'As far as I can see, it will be her bearing the brunt of this, so the least we can do is to make things as easy as possible for them both.'

Francesca flashed him a grateful look but Malcolm still looked doubtful. 'Ros and the other girls know, don't they?' He looked from Francesca to David.

David nodded. 'That doesn't bother me. I'd stake my life on our girls when it comes to confidentiality.'

'Well, yes, of course.' Malcolm had the grace to look shamefaced.

'I felt they had to be told,' David went on. 'They

know Guy too well and they would have been sure to notice something was amiss, but individual patients would have only seen him at the most, I would say, two or three times during the last few months, so provided he studies their case histories I feel sure he could get through.'

'What about recent medical updates—drugs, treatments et cetera?' Malcolm still looked dubious.

'He only has to read back copies of the medical journals to cover the period he's lost,' said Francesca eagerly, and when Malcolm didn't reply she went on, 'and let's face it, that's what the rest of us do all the time to keep up to date.'

'She has a point, Malcolm,' said David.

Still Malcolm remained silent and Francesca's heart sank. If she failed to convince her two partners that Guy was fit to practise, heaven only knew what would happen. In the end, in desperation, she said, 'Won't you talk to him, judge for yourselves just how much he can remember. . .?'

'I was just going to suggest the same thing,' said David. 'I think we should see Guy, Malcolm, and talk to him before we make any decisions.'

'Very well.' At last Malcolm nodded and Francesca gave an inward sigh of relief.

'If that goes well,' said David, 'I suggest Guy should have a definite period of catching up before he starts practising again. He could, for example, go into the clinic each day to familiarise himself with the place. He could then spend time reading and catching up on the journals and periodicals. What do you think, Fran?'

She nodded. 'That sounds fine. . .thank you, thank you both.'

Malcolm shrugged, then stared curiously at her. 'How the hell are you coping?' he asked bluntly.

'It isn't easy.' She grimaced. 'But I shall persevere. I'm just living one day at a time and hoping that his memory will eventually return. The doctor who treated him in Spain said if I kept everything as normal as possible. . .it might gradually come back to him.'

'And he doesn't remember you at all?' Malcolm stared at her as if appalled by the notion.

She shook her head. 'No,' she said quietly.

'So what's the last thing he does remember?'

'Being in America.'

'Good grief!' Malcolm looked shocked. 'The poor chap, he must wonder what the hell he's doing here in the Lake District.' He frowned as if deliberating, then said, 'I know that doctor told you to keep everything normal, Francesca, but don't put too much pressure on him, will you?'

'Of course not. . .'

'Might do more harm than good.' Malcolm stood up. 'Well, this won't do. Sarah will be wondering where I've got to. Tell Guy to come and see us. . .say, tomorrow lunchtime?' He raised his eyebrows at David, who nodded in reply. 'See you both.' With an absent-minded wave of his hand he strode out of the kitchen.

Francesca and David continued to sit at the table, then after a while, David said quietly, 'He's right, you know.'

'What do you mean?' Francesca looked up sharply.

'About not putting Guy under too much pressure. The mind's a funny thing.'

'I know. I know. . .' To her horror she felt her voice begin to shake. 'He. . .he doesn't even know me, David,' she whispered. 'You have no idea, his eyes are just blank when he looks at me, it's as if he's a stranger. . .no, it's even worse than that because at least a stranger might show interest in meeting someone. . .but with Guy. . .' She broke off in distress.

'Give him time,' said David gently, 'just give him time.'

'But supposing he never remembers. . .never remembers meeting me, marrying me. . .?'

'Come on, Fran, this isn't like you.' David stood up. 'You are usually the positive one. Tell yourself that gradually he will remember and when he does you'll be there to witness the moment...to share it with him...just think, it could be like falling in love all over again.' There was a faintly rueful note in his voice and as he was speaking he moved round behind her chair and lightly placed a comforting hand on her shoulder.

There was silence for a moment, then Francesca said, 'I'm sorry, David, the last month can't have been too easy for you either.'

He withdrew his hand and stepped back. 'Oh, I'm a survivor and a bit of a realist...I knew the moment I saw you and Guy together any chance I thought I might have had was long gone.'

'Even so...' Francesca's unspoken words adequately summed up her feelings and David gave a short laugh.

'It was my own fault,' he said wryly, leaning back against the large Welsh dresser that took up an entire wall of his kitchen. 'I should have thought twice about asking him to come here to do locum—I might have known what would happen. Guy always was a charmer.'

Suddenly Francesca longed to ask David if he knew about Chloe, who she was, where she had fitted into Guy's past and what she had meant to him. Instead, her courage failed her and abruptly she stood up. 'I must be going,' she said.

David looked up sharply. 'Oh, right,' he said as if for the moment he'd forgotten why she was there. 'Yes, of course.'

'Thank you, David,' she said and her tone softened. 'Thank you for being so understanding.'

'Don't thank me.' He shrugged and moved away from the dresser. 'In the end it's all going to be down to that husband of yours to prove that he can cope.'

'I would think Guy will be as grateful as me to know that you are giving him the chance,' she replied.

'So I'm to be on trial.'

It was the next afternoon and Francesca had

returned to the cottage to see Guy following his lunchtime meeting with the other two partners.

'Of course you're not!' Her heart sank at his tone.

'So what would you call it?' He was sitting in the garden and he looked up at her, shading his eyes from the surprisingly warm September sun.

'Simply a time of catching up,' she replied firmly ignoring the slightly sarcastic note in his voice. 'A time of reading journals, familiarising yourself with the patients and their medical conditions.'

'And of attending lectures at the postgrad centre at the hospital. . .?'

'Yes.' She paused 'Whose idea was that?'

'Whose do you think?'

'Malcolm's?'

'Who else's?' Guy paused. 'He seems to have less faith in me than anyone.'

'I'm sure he has faith in you, Guy. . .' Francesca bit her lip.

'Are you?' He raised one eyebrow, the gesture sardonic now, and when she gave a helpless shrug he gave a short, bitter laugh. 'Oh, don't get me wrong,' he said, 'I don't blame him. It's like I said before, if it were the other way round I wouldn't be too keen to take a chance on me either.'

'There's no problem with David,' Francesca said stoutly.

'Well, there wouldn't be, would there?' He got to his feet.

'What do you mean?' Frowning, she watched as he folded the garden chair he had been sitting on.

'David's a nice guy. . .' he said over his shoulder.

'Yes, he is. . .' Francesca, suddenly wary at something in his tone, watched as he stacked the chair along with two others in the glass lean-to beside the back door.

'We go back a long way. . .' Guy straightened up and studied his hands, which had become soiled with some particles of rust from the metal frame of the chair.

'That's true. . .'

'And he quite obviously thinks the world of you,' he concluded softly, wiping his hands down the sides of his jeans.

Francesca stared at him and to her dismay felt her cheeks colour. She took a deep breath, aware that Guy had noticed her spontaneous reaction. 'David is a good friend,' she said firmly. 'A good friend to us both.'

'He's also, as far as I can make out, the only person who calls you Fran. . .'

'David has always called me Fran,' she replied calmly.

'And you don't mind?' he asked. 'I wouldn't have thought you'd like your name abbreviated.'

'I don't usually,' she agreed then added, 'But it's different with David.'

'Really?'

'Yes.' Once more, to her annoyance, she felt her cheeks colour and to hide the fact she turned and began to walk back into the cottage. 'There was a bit of a song and dance about it when we first met, but I gave in in the end,' she called over her shoulder. 'But honestly, Guy, all David wants is to see things get back to normal,' she continued, 'And as to the suggestion of a catching-up period for you,' she added as Guy followed her indoors, 'well, I think that's an excellent idea.'

'Provided it works,' Guy replied cryptically.

Francesca paused and looked back. 'What do you mean?' She frowned. 'Provided it works?'

'What I say. It'll be fine at the end of this period, however long they're planning on, if I've managed to catch up with all I've forgotten, but what happens if I can't?'

'I don't understand.'

'What if I'm unable to retain anything new? What if my short-term memory has become permanently impaired? Will your partners then decide I would be not only a risk, but also a liability, and kick me out of the practice?'

'Oh, Guy!' She stared at him, then in sudden

exasperation she said, 'For goodness' sake...stop creating difficulties! Here we are, trying to make things as easy as possible for you——'

'Don't you mean trying to humour me,' he cut her short, 'in case I have some sort of brainstorm...isn't that more like it?' There was a half-smile on his lips as he spoke but Francesca was only too aware of the desperation behind his words.

'Of course not!' she cried. Then more quietly she repeated, 'Of course not, Guy. We all care about you...the other two are your partners, as well as your friends...they care...and I...I'm your wife...and I care...I care...because...because...I love you!' Her voice broke and with a sob she turned and with her head down hurried away from him through the cottage and up the stairs.

In their bedroom, with her hands clenched into tight, angry fists and fighting her tears, she sat on the bed, the bed where last night once again they had slept; together, but apart.

After her conversation the previous evening with Malcolm and David she had wondered if sleeping in the same bed as Guy could constitute putting too much pressure on him—pressure to resume a sexual relationship he knew nothing about—but in the end she had preferred to take Helen Ryder's advice, and indeed to follow her own intuition, and keep everything as normal as possible. And she had come to the conclusion that if she suggested Guy sleep in the spare room he might well see it as rejection instead of an attempt to give him space.

Now she wondered. Maybe he did need space, time on his own. Maybe she was trying too hard, maybe they were all trying too hard. Perhaps they should just leave Guy to himself.

'I'm sorry.'

She looked up sharply. He was standing in the doorway, watching her.

'It's OK.' Swiftly she brushed her hand across her face.

'You've been crying.'

'No, no, I haven't.' Briskly she stood up.

'Yes, you have, and it's all my fault. I'm a selfish, ungrateful brute and I really am sorry.' He barred her path as she would have left the room and before she knew what was happening he had taken hold of her arms.

She stiffened involuntarily and they stared at each other in helpless despair. Apart from the moment in Spain in the villa when he had examined her shoulder, it was the first time he had touched her since the accident.

She stood rigid, wondering what he would do next.

He continued to hold her and she lowered her head, unable to meet his gaze any longer. Then she felt his arms go round her and for the briefest of moments he held her close. She caught her breath, longing to hold him in turn but not daring to.

'Thank you for being so understanding,' he murmured against the dark tangle of her hair.

'I'm trying,' she whispered. 'Believe me, Guy, it isn't easy, but I'm trying.'

He held her for a further moment then released her. It had hardly been a lovers' embrace, more one of comfort between friends, but it was better than nothing, and perhaps, Francesca thought, it was a start.

She had to go then to complete her house calls, but when she returned that evening she found he had prepared a meal for them both.

'I don't know your tastes in food,' he said as they began to eat, 'but I raided your store-cupboards and made a calculated guess.'

'A very good guess,' she said; 'this curry is delicious.'

'That's something I haven't forgotten,' he grinned; 'how to make a decent curry.'

And later, when she had showered and was sitting in bed reading and he came into the bedroom, she looked at him over the top of her book and said, 'Guy, would you be happier sleeping in the spare room?'

He turned from the wardrobe and looked at her.

'Would you be happier if I slept in the spare room?'

She shook her head.

As he climbed into bed beside her he said, 'I'll come to the clinic with you in the morning and start my catching-up process.'

She gave an inward sigh of relief and closed her book.

'But first, maybe I could do a bit of genning up. What did you say those receptionists' names were?' he asked as he turned out the light.

In the darkness Francesca smiled. 'Well, there's Ros,' she began, 'she's the practice manager; then there's Marie, our secretary; then there's Fiona, and Sue. . .'

There was a definite touch of autumn in the air the following morning as they set out for the clinic in Francesca's car.

'Don't I have a car?' asked Guy as he took his place beside her.

'Why do you ask?' She threw him a sidelong glance as he fastened his seatbelt, thinking how fit and tanned he looked after his days in the Spanish sun.

'Well, quite apart from the fact that I've always been something of a car fanatic, I would have thought I'd needed one if I'd been doing my share of house calls. . .I take it I was doing my share?' he asked when she didn't immediately answer.

'Oh, yes,' she replied, 'you did your share, more than your share at times. You had a hire-car when you first arrived, then. . .then you used the Land Rover.'

'Land Rover?' he said quickly.

'Yes.' She threw him another glance. 'Why do you say it like that?'

'Nothing. . .it's just that I saw a Land Rover in the car park yesterday—is that the one I've been using?'

'It is.' She paused. 'You don't remember anything else about it?'

'No.' He was still frowning. 'Why?'

'Oh, it was nothing,' she said lightly, 'nothing at all.' Just for one crazy moment there she had wondered if he had remembered their first meeting, that day in the snow when she had nearly run him over with the Land Rover. 'Actually,' she said quickly, 'you have a new car on order.'

'Have I?'

She smiled as she dectected the eagerness in his voice, then as they approached the busy shopping centre she turned her attention to the early-morning traffic. On the corner outside the Methodist chapel a group of women and children were waiting to cross the road. As Francesca drove by two of the women waved.

'Wave back,' Francesca said quickly.

'I know them?' asked Guy through the side of his mouth, at the same time obediently waving to the group.

'Yes, all of them. You helped deliver the tall woman's baby and you treated the little ginger-haired boy when he had chickenpox.'

'I've an awful feeling this is all going to be a lot more difficult than I feared,' he groaned as they swept into the clinic car park.

'Nonsense,' Francesca replied with more conviction than she was feeling, 'you'll sail through. Just be yourself.'

'So what's the make of this car I have on order?' he said, making no attempt to open the door as Francesca switched off the engine.

'Wait and see,' she replied lightly, climbing out of the car, opening the rear door and dragging her medical case from the back seat.

'Oh, come on,' he protested as he too at last climbed from the car and slammed the door, 'tell me.'

'No,' she said firmly, 'it can be a surprise. You'll just have to be patient.'

'It isn't fair,' he protested as they crossed the car park, 'you have an ongoing advantage over me, knowing things about me that I don't know myself.'

'It'll keep you on your toes!' She pulled a face at

him and by the time they pushed open the double doors they were both laughing.

David and Ros were standing in front of the reception desk in deep conversation. They sprang apart when they caught sight of Guy and herself, and Francesca had the distinct impression that not only had they been discussing them but also that they were amazed to see them laughing.

'Hello,' a welcoming smile quickly lit Ros's face, 'we were just talking about you two,' she admitted.

'You were?' Francesca felt herself tense and didn't dare look at Guy. His mood had been light-hearted only seconds before, but she had already learnt how that could change in the bat of an eyelid.

'Yes,' Ros went on easily, 'I was just telling David I've sorted out all the material for Guy to read. It's upstairs in the library, together with a full coffee-pot.' She smiled at Guy, and, to Francesca's relief, he smiled back.

With Guy safely esconced in the library Francesca went to her consulting-room and prepared to begin her morning surgery.

After glancing through her mountain of post, already sifted by Ros, and knowing it would require her closer attention later, she pressed the buzzer on her desk to indicate to the receptionists on duty that she was ready for her first patient.

However, when the door opened a moment later it was Ros who stood on the threshold and not the patient she was expecting.

'Just checking you're OK.' Ros's smile was sympathetic.

'Yes, Ros, I'm fine.' Francesca sighed. 'At least, I think I am. Most of the time I feel I'm walking on eggshells, but,' she shrugged, 'I keep reminding myself it must be worse for Guy.'

'I'm not sure that it is,' Ros replied thoughtfully, stepping right into the room and shutting the door behind her. She was small and fair skinned with wispy fair hair that was always escaping from the tortoiseshell slide at the nape of her neck. 'It must be hell for you,' she said.

Francesca stared at her. She and Ros had known each other for a long time and they understood each other well. With another sigh, Francesca covered her face with her hands, wincing as the movement caused a pain to shoot through her bruised shoulder. 'Yes, it is,' she admitted at last through her fingers. 'And do you know the worst part?' Lowering her hands, she looked up at Ros, who shook her head. 'It's when Guy looks at me sometimes and I wonder if he's wondering what he saw in me and why on earth he married me.'

'Come on, now, stop it, Francesca,' said Ros firmly. 'He wouldn't be thinking anything of the sort.' She paused and tucked a strand of hair behind her ear. 'If anything, he's probably marvelling at his luck and wondering why you agreed to take him on.'

Francesca managed a weak smile then shook her head helplessly. 'Thanks, Ros,' she said, then, sitting up straight, she squared her shoulders. 'Ah, well,' she said briskly, 'I suppose I've just got to get on with it—I don't really have much choice. . .'

'What are the chances of his regaining his memory?' asked Ros curiously.

'Pretty good, actually.' Francesca nodded. 'Probably not all at once, and maybe not for some time, but perhaps gradually. . .who knows?'

'It could be worse. . .' Ros began, although her expression betrayed that she doubted it.

'Oh, it could definitely be worse,' replied Ros. 'I thought at first he might have broken his neck—can you imagine Guy in a wheelchair?'

Ros stared at her then as the awful prospect registered she raised her eyes heavenwards. 'Hmm,' she agreed, 'you're right, it most definitely could have been worse.' She paused, as if searching for the right words. 'But we wanted you to know, Francesca, and that includes the other girls, we'll do all we can to help, and I guarantee, no one need ever know.'

'Thanks, Ros.' Francesca swallowed, conscious of a

lump that had just risen in her throat. 'Everyone's been marvellous and I really do appreciate it.'

'Don't mention it.' Ros smiled and turned to the door. 'I'm going to sort out the records of the patients that Guy saw while he was locum, so that he can gen up in case he has to see them again.' She opened the door, then paused. 'Shall I send your first patient in?'

Francesca nodded. 'Yes, I think the sooner I get back into the swing of things the better. . .oh, but Ros, before you go. . .how's your mother?'

Ros paused, one hand on the door handle. 'Not too good at the moment. She gets so confused at times.'

'How did she get on at the day centre?'

Ros shook her head. 'She didn't like it. She prefers to stay at home but it isn't always easy getting people to keep an eye on her when I'm not there. . .it's not everyone who understands the nature of Alzheimer's disease.'

'It must be very difficult for you,' said Francesca. 'Let me know if there's anything else I can do to help.'

'You do enough as it is,' replied Ros. 'It can't be everyone who has such an understanding GP,' she added as she went out of the room, shutting the door behind her.

Getting back into the swing of things proved to be a little more difficult than Francesca had imagined, for almost every patient she saw wanted to talk about the wedding and ask whether she had enjoyed her honeymoon. Even Jean Blake, who came in for a routine cervical smear and breast examination, wanted to know all about the villa.

'Did it have its own pool?' she asked during the examination.

Francesca nodded. 'It did, and the weather was hot, even hotter than usual for Spain in September.'

'That's what I could do with,' Jean sighed, 'a bit of hot sun.'

'Couldn't you get away?' asked Francesca as she slipped the smear slide into a container ready for the laboratory.

'Oh, I dare say we could get away if we really put our minds to it.' Jean grimaced and, getting down from the couch, began to get dressed. 'no, it isn't that, it's Jeff.'

'Jeff?' By this time Francesca was washing her hands in the basin on the far side of her consulting-room, but she turned her head in surprise at Jean's words. 'It's not his heart again, is it?'

'Oh, no, it's nothing like that,' said Jean quickly, 'he's been fine since that last scare, really he has. It's just that he doesn't like leaving the farm—or being away from home for that matter.'

'But now you have a manager I would have thought it would be easier for you to get away, and besides,' said Francesca wiping her hands on a paper towel, 'it does everyone good to have the occasional break.'

'I know that,' said Jean, 'but you try telling my husband. I don't somehow think he'd agree. . .on the other hand, you know what these men are, if you were to let him think it was his idea. . .' She winked and Francesca laughed.

'I might just do that,' she said, then, growing serious again, she told her, 'Give us a ring, Jean, in about three weeks for your smear result.'

'I will, and thank you, Doctor.'

Francesca opened the door for Jean and followed her into the passage. 'I think you're my last patient,' she said. 'It's time I went in search of some coffee.'

At the reception desk Marie, the practice secretary, was talking to a man with a shock of frizzy blond hair. As he turned, Francesca realised it was the photographer who had taken her wedding photographs.

'Hello, Marcus,' she said, waving a hand in farewell to Jean Blake as she went out of the front door, 'have you brought my photographs?'

The photographer grinned, displaying a gold tooth. 'I have,' he said then, correcting himself, added, 'Well, the proofs, not the actual photographs. Came out a treat, they did, even if I do say so myself.'

'Good.' Francesca smiled, waiting, then, realising

his hands were empty, said, 'So where are they?'

'Oh.' He had been leaning against the desk but he straightened up, almost sending a potted cactus skimming off the polished surface. 'I gave them to your husband,' he said.

'My husband. . .?' Her heart gave a leap of alarm.

'Yes, he was here when I came in,' said Marcus. 'He said you were doing your surgery so I gave him the photos. . .' He frowned. 'That was OK, wasn't it?' A wary look had come into his eyes.

'Oh, yes,' replied Francesca quickly, not wanting him to even suspect there might be a problem, 'yes, of course it was.'

'Good.' The man looked relieved, then, glancing uncertainly at Marie, he said, 'Well, this won't do, I must get on. Let me have your order, Dr Sinclair, when you've chosen what you want. . .and don't forget, I do a very good deal if you have the padded leather album. . . Cheerio, Marie.' With a wave of his hand he was gone, bounding out of the swing doors and almost colliding with a patient supported by arm crutches who was coming in.

'Was that all right?' asked Marie anxiously as they watched him go. 'Your husband was here and Marcus had handed over the package before I realised what had happened.'

'It's OK, Marie,' said Francesca, more calmly than she was feeling. 'Where did Guy go?' she asked after a pause.

'As far as I know,' the secretary replied, 'he went back to the library. . .' A frown creased her forehead. 'Do you think. . .?'

But Francesca didn't give the secretary time to voice any fears the effect of seeing his wedding photos might have on Guy's memory. Instead, she took the stairs two at a time and as she flung open the library door her heart was thudding.

Guy was sitting on an easy-chair. Before him on a low coffee-table were spread at least a dozen proofs. It was obvious that he had been looking through them and when he looked up to see who had burst into the room he still had a smile on his face.

Francesca froze in the doorway, her gaze travelling from his face to the photographs then back to his face again.

'Oh, good, it's you,' he said calmly. 'Apparently, these are our wedding photographs.'

'Yes. . .' She held her breath.

'They are very good.' He picked up one, holding it so the light played on their faces. 'This one especially.' He held it at arm's length. She stared at him, her mind in turmoil. 'Yes,' he went on slowly, 'they're very good. . .'

'But do you remember. . .?' She managed to find the words at last. 'Do you recall their being taken? The day itself. . .?'

He glanced up at her and for a moment she could have sworn there was something in his eyes, something to suggest he did remember, then to her dismay he shook his head.

'But. . .I thought. . .' her heart sank '. . .hoped. . . Oh, I don't know what I hoped, but when I came in you were smiling, Guy. . .you were smiling as you were looking at the photos. . .so what were you thinking?' she asked in a sudden rush of emotion.

He looked up again, the photograph still in his hand. 'I was simply wondering,' he said, 'how I ever persuaded such a lovely lady to marry me.'

CHAPTER SEVEN

AT HIS words Francesca felt a ridiculous surge of pleasure and at the same time was aware that the blood had rushed to her cheeks. Helplessly she stood in the open doorway, watching him as he continued to study the photographs, holding up first one then another for closer inspection. By calling her lovely he had at least dispelled the fear she'd had that he might be wondering what he had seen in her.

He looked up again then and, oblivious to the significance of what he had said, appeared surprised that she was still standing in the doorway.

'Don't you want to see them?' he asked.

'Yes,' Francesca summoned her concentration, 'yes, of course.' Briskly she crossed the room and took a couple of the photographs that he handed up to her. She had to steel herself to look at them, aware that Guy was watching her, waiting for her reaction.

The first one was of herself and her father arriving at the church. The nineteen-twenties-style dress that she had chosen with so much care looked good and the beaded satin cap, while covering her unruly dark hair, somehow managed to accentuate the delicacy of her features. Her father, resplendent in his morning suit, was smiling proudly at the camera.

'Your father. . .?' asked Guy quietly.

'Yes. . .' She nodded, unable to say more, then quickly she looked at the second photograph. This was of herself and Guy leaving the church in a flurry of confetti. They were both laughing, herself at someone just out of the camera's view and Guy, happily, tenderly, looking down at her.

She swallowed, and for the briefest of moments closed her eyes.

When she opened them again Guy was sifting

through the rest of the photographs on the table as if he was searching for something.

Without a word Francesca knelt down beside the table and began picking up the rest of the photographs one by one and studying them.

While they had been on honeymoon, before the accident, she had looked forward to this moment so much, but now that it had come it was bitter-sweet.

'Lavinia,' said Guy, pointing to a photograph of the guests in the hotel grounds at Windermere.

'Yes,' she nodded, 'your sister. . .'

'She came?' He sounded surprised.

'You didn't think she would have been there?'

He shrugged. 'Yes. . .I suppose so. . .it's just that I haven't seen her for a long time. . .I thought I might have remembered if she was there. . .' He trailed off, shaking his head.

Francesca watched him, longing to help him but not knowing how.

'Henry?' he asked suddenly, sifting more urgently through the pictures.

'Your brother?'

'Yes, was he there?'

'No, she said quickly, 'he couldn't come—he's abroad. . .the Antarctic, I think.'

He nodded slowly, frowning, the concentration deep. 'He's a marine biologist. . .' he said at last, then looked up sharply as if craving her reassurance that he had at least got something right.

'Yes, yes,' she nodded quickly, 'yes, that's right.'

He took a deep breath that could almost have been a sigh of relief then, returning to the photographs, he said, 'So did I have anyone else there?'

'Your uncle—Uncle George.'

'Uncle George?' He looked incredulous. 'Uncle George came?'

'Yes. . .' She found herself smiling at his expression. 'Why. . .?'

'The old devil. . .' He chuckled, shaking his head. 'Anyone else?'

'Lavinia's husband Ronald.' Leaning forward, she pointed to a tall thin man at the back of one of the group photographs.

Narrowing his eyes, Guy moved closer for a better look, so close that his face was only a couple of inches from her own.

Slowly, carefully, she moved her head. It would be so easy to touch his lips with hers. But how would he react? Maybe she should just do it and see.

'Ronald's an absolute prat,' he said with a sudden guffaw of laughter.

Abruptly Francesca moved back, the moment gone. 'That's not a very nice thing to say about your brother-in-law,' she said quickly, the mock-severity in her tone attempting to conceal her own tangled feelings.

'Maybe not. But it happens to be true. I never could fathom out what Livvy saw in him in the first place.'

'Well, she must have seen something,' Francesca replied briskly, scrambling to her feet, 'otherwise she wouldn't have married him.'

'Just as you must have seen something,' he said lightly, looking up at her, a half-smile on his features, 'or presumably you wouldn't have married me.'

'Absolutely,' she replied, equally lightly, then, not giving him further chance to speculate, went on hurriedly, 'How did you get on this morning?' As she spoke she indicated the pile of papers and journals on the desk by the window and the sets of patients' records that Ros had sorted out and placed in two cardboard boxes.

'You mean my revision?' he said, looking up from the photographs almost reluctantly as if he'd had to tear his gaze away.

She nodded. 'Was it too difficult?'

'Not really, no. A couple of breakthroughs on the drugs scene surprised me—not so much the drugs themselves but the actual pharmaceutical companies who made the breakthrough...apart from that,' he shrugged and stood up, 'it was quite easy reading—nothing too taxing at all.'

'But nothing significant either?' As she spoke Francesca crossed to the coffee machine and poured two mugs of coffee. 'How about the patient records?'

Guy didn't answer and, picking up the mugs, she turned to him to see why. She was about to repeat the question then realised that Guy was standing in the middle of the room, staring at the mugs of coffee in her hands. There was a strange expression on his face.

'What is it?' she said and her voice came out as barely more than a whisper.

'Black...as it comes,' he muttered, continuing to stare at the steaming mugs of coffee.

'Yes, I know.' She frowned and glanced down at the mugs. When she looked up again he was still staring as if he was in some sort of trance. Francesca felt a shiver run down her spine. There was something fey, almost ethereal about the look in his grey eyes.

'Guy?' She swallowed. 'What is it?'

He moved his gaze then from the mugs to her face and stared blankly at her. 'I don't know,' he said and his expression, although bewildered, was normal again. 'I'm not sure...a sense of *déjà vu*, I think...of having lived that moment before...'

'A lifting of the curtain?' she asked softly.

'I don't know.' Shaking his head, he took his coffee. 'Perhaps. But whatever it was, it's gone now.' He glanced at her. 'You were saying something?' he asked.

She stared at him, reluctant to let the moment slip away if there was a chance he might have remembered something, but Guy clearly didn't want to prolong the incident. 'I was simply asking about the patient records,' she said at last.

'I haven't really started on them yet,' he replied. 'I just glanced at a few—they didn't mean a thing,' he added quickly before she could ask, 'but one thing that did strike me,' he went on, glancing down at the two boxes of records on the floor, 'was that I don't seem to have seen that many patients in the period of time I've been here.'

'Oh, you have,' said Francesca quickly, 'but many

of the people you saw were temporary residents, people on holiday here—they just filled in forms to which you would have added details of their treatment, then the forms would have been returned to their own GPs.'

'Of course!' His face cleared. 'Before I went to the States most of my work was in hospitals—I've done very little general practice, and I wasn't used to that particular procedure. I was beginning to think I hadn't been pulling my weight.'

'You more than did that,' Francesca replied. 'Why do you think we wanted you as a partner?'

He shrugged and at the lost, helpless expression on his face she longed to hug him. His gaze flickered to the photographs again. 'This church. . .' he began, pointing to the building behind the groups of smiling people.

'Yes?' She looked up eagerly, hoping something else might be penetrating the mist in his mind.

'Where is it?'

She gave a small sigh. 'Here,' she said, 'in Bletchley Bridge.'

'Really?' Yet again he seemed surprised. 'And my best man?' he asked a moment later, looking down at the pictures and beginning to sift through them again.

'It was David,' Francesca replied.

'David.'

'He was the obvious choice. Your brother couldn't be here. Your lifelong friend John was in India and you and David. . .well, you do go back a long way.'

'Yes, I know. . .' He hesitated.

'You seem surprised that you should have chosen David.' She frowned. 'Why?'

'I don't know. . .I can't explain it——' He broke off as the library door opened and David himself appeared.

'Hello, you two.' He stood in the doorway for a moment as if afraid of intruding, his gaze flickering from Francesca to Guy then back to Francesca. 'Am I interrupting something?'

'Of course not, David,' Francesca replied firmly. 'Come on in. We were looking at our wedding photographs. Would you like to see them?'

'Oh, yes, rather.' Crossing the room, David took the pile of photographs that Francesca picked up from the table.

They stood watching as he leafed through the pictures, smiling at some, studying others more closely.

'I say,' he said at last, 'they're awfully good, aren't they? Marcus really has surpassed himself this time—and your worries about your dress really were groundless, Fran; you look absolutely gorgeous, if your husband doesn't mind my saying so.' He grinned at Guy, whose expression remained inscrutable; then he grew serious. 'These haven't helped?' He indicated the photographs.

'Afraid not.' It was Francesca who answered, hastily taking the photographs from David and pushing them into their wallet. 'Still, never mind. . .'

As if he sensed tension David turned to Guy and, changing the subject, said, 'How did you get on this morning?'

'You mean with my revision homework?' asked Guy, the sarcasm in his voice only too apparent. In the silence that followed, his remark must have sounded petty even to him, for he had the grace to look shamefaced. 'Oh, it was OK,' he muttered at last. 'Not too many startling medical breakthroughs, were there?'

'You can say that again.' David pulled a face, then, glancing at his watch, said, 'Well, this is all very pleasant but it's not getting my house calls done—I'll see you both later.'

As David left the library Francesca said, 'I must go too, Guy. . .' She paused, hesitating. 'I would think you've had enough of that today.' She nodded towards the journals. 'Would you like to come with me?'

'Won't people find that strange?'

'I don't see why,' she replied calmly. 'People know we are married but that you're not officially a partner yet, and besides, from your point of view it will help to familiarise you with the locality. What do you say?' She looked hopefully at him, noting his dubious expression but desperately wanting him to say he would come with her.

'All right,' he said at last, then with a wry grin he added, 'Lead on, Dr Sinclair.' It was the first time he'd called her that since the accident and she felt a brief, crazy surge of pleasure.

For the first three house calls Guy chose to remain in the car, but on the fourth call the decision was made for him.

'I've a couple of patients to see in here,' said Francesca as she left the Bowness road, drove in through a large pair of white gates and up a short drive lined with rhododendron bushes. She brought the car to a halt before a pleasant brick house with double-fronted bay windows. A noticeboard set in a bed of fading blue hydrangeas stated that the building was The Peacehaven Residential Home.

Francesca glanced at Guy, wondering if he recognised the place, knowing he had visited it several times during the summer. 'Do you want to come in with me?' she asked.

Before he had the chance to answer there came a sudden knock on the window on Guy's side of the car. Guy looked up sharply and Francesca leaned forward. An elderly man, with thick white hair protruding from beneath a tweed cap, was leaning heavily on a walking-stick and peering through the window.

'So you're back, then,' the man shouted, at the same time indicating for Guy to open the door or at least wind down the window. 'I heard you were back.'

'Who is he?' Guy threw Francesca a frantic glance.

'Percy,' she replied quickly out of the side of her mouth. 'Percy Masters. He's eighty-four, has lived here for years. He's a retired gardener and thinks the gardens here are his responsibility.'

'Medical history?' Guy demanded, one hand on the door catch.

'Very few problems—apart from arthritis, mainly in his hands and his knees.'

'Thanks.' Guy opened the car door. 'Hello, Percy,' he said easily. 'How are you?' He stepped out of the car and looked round the neatly tended flower borders surrounding the lawns. 'Those chrysanthemums look a treat,' he said, 'they're a credit to you.'

Francesca smiled at his quick thinking and opened her own door.

'Aye,' Percy pushed his cap back and scratched his head, 'not so bad, are they—even if I do say so meself?'

'They're beautiful, Percy.' Francesca joined in as she too climbed out of the car. 'That copper colour is my favourite.'

'Have a good holiday, did you?' Percy peered at them both then, not giving them a chance to answer, said, 'I don't hold with all this foreign travel meself. Don't know why you couldn't have stayed here—finest scenery in the world, and a darn sight safer, I'll be bound.'

'You could well be right.' Francesca glanced at Guy, who gave a rueful nod.

'You come to see Em?' asked Percy.

Guy glanced at Francesca, who quickly said, 'That's right, Percy.'

'She been bad again—coughing all night, she was; we could all hear her,' Percy muttered, turning to follow Francesca into the house.

Guy settled himself against the bonnet of the car and folded his arms, preparing to wait for Francesca, but Percy turned and glared at him. 'Aren't you coming in too?' he barked.

'I'm sure my wife can cope,' replied Guy.

'But Em'll want to see you as well. We'd never hear the last of it if she knew you'd been here and hadn't been in to see her.'

Guy took a deep breath. 'In that case. . .' He pushed himself away from the car and, ignoring Francesca's amused expression, followed Percy into the house.

They were met in the hall by Maureen Fellows, the matron, who also expressed her delight at seeing the pair of them. She, however, seemed more envious of their Spanish holiday than Percy had been.

'Just what I could do with,' she said, 'a couple of weeks in the sun.' She paused. 'While one of you sees Em do you think the other could nip in and see Walter?'

'We'll both go in to Em,' said Francesca quickly, 'then I'll leave Guy to chat to her while I see Walter. Is it his prostate playing up again?'

'Yes, I'm afraid it is—it looks as if it will come to that operation you were talking about, but it's Em I'm really worried about.' Maureen led the way down the hall then stopped and tapped lightly on a door that stood ajar before pushing it right open. 'Em, my love,' she said to someone inside the room, 'guess who's here to see you.'

Emily Addison, who, like Percy, was well into her eighties, was sitting in a high-backed chair by the window. She looked round as they came into the room and Francesca smiled when she saw that in spite of the fact that the old lady was not feeling well she was wearing bright pink lipstick, face powder and blue eye-shadow. Round her neck she wore two strands of pearls and in her ears drop pearl earrings. Her faded blue eyes gleamed when she caught sight of Guy.

'So you got back from your honeymoon,' she said and her voice was deep and, although shaky, resonant, the articulation perfect.

'Yes, Em,' replied Guy, rising to the occasion. 'We got back and I said to Francesca, the first thing I must do is go and see Em.'

'Liar!' the old lady retorted but she looked pleased. Then as Francesca opened her case the lines on Em's forehead deepened. 'What's all this Em business?' she demanded suddenly, glaring at Guy.

'I'm sorry?' Guy frowned and shot Francesca a quick glance but she was forced to shake her head, unable to help him.

'What happened to "Duchess"?' There was a peevish note in Em's voice now.

'Duchess?' Guy, playing for time, picked up a photograph from the dressing-table and began studying it.

Looking over his shoulder, Francesca saw it was of a beautiful young girl in a scanty costume edged with sequins and feathers.

'You always called me Duchess whenever you came here before,' retorted Em. 'I suppose getting married has put paid to all that...too familiar, I suppose.' She shot Francesca a scathing look.

Guy laughed. 'Of course it isn't; if you still want me to call you Duchess then that's exactly what I'll call you.' Leaning forward, he planted a kiss on Em's powdered cheek.

'There's no need for that, young man,' she said crisply but she looked pleased all the same.

'Now, Em,' said Francesca, 'I understand from Matron your chest has been playing you up again—I think,' she added taking her stethoscope from her case, 'you'd better let me have a listen.'

While Guy strolled to the window and proceeded to study the photograph more closely Francesca unbuttoned Em's blouse, positioned the stethoscope and listened to her chest.

'Your chest is rather congested, Em,' she said at last. 'I'm going to give you a course of antibiotics.' Slipping her stethoscope back into her case, she drew out a prescription pad and scribbled out the necessary medication. 'Hopefully you'll soon be feeling a lot better,' she said, tearing off the page. 'Now,' Francesca stood up, 'I'll leave my husband here to chat to you for a few minutes while I call on another of the residents.'

'You mean Walter?' said Em. 'His waterworks have been playing up again...in and out that lavatory every few minutes, he is.'

Feeling her lips twitch and not daring to meet Guy's gaze, Francesca handed Em's prescription to Maureen and followed her from the room.

'I'm sure people just think I'm being rude,' Guy said

a little later as they drove away from Peacehaven.

'I don't think they do,' replied Francesca, waving to Percy, who had presented her with a huge bunch of copper chrysanthemums as she left the house and was now standing on the drive watching them go. 'They probably just think you're a bit absentminded, and we doctors do seem to have acquired that reputation anyway—so I shouldn't worry. Besides, you handled things very well with Em.'

'What a character!' He half turned to Francesca. 'I gather that was her in the photograph?'

'Yes,' Francesca nodded, 'she spent all her life in the theatre; when that photograph was taken she was with the Folies Bergère in Paris.'

They fell silent for a moment, each reflecting on the old lady, then Francesca said, 'Her emphysema was bad today and a further chest infection has set in. She doesn't let on, but she's really quite poorly. . .of course, she's been a lifelong smoker. . .' She paused as she realised something had taken Guy's attention. 'What is it?' she asked, taking her eyes from the road for a moment.

'That church. . .over there,' he pointed, 'isn't that where. . .where we were married?'

'It is. . . Do you. . .?'

'I recognise it from the photographs,' he said quickly.

'Oh, I see.' For one crazy moment Francesca had thought he had remembered it.

'Do you think it will be open?'

'I don't know. . .probably, there are still a lot of tourists around.' She hesitated, putting her foot on the brake. 'Do you want to go and see?'

'Yes. . .' He too sounded hesitant as if he was afraid he might regret this decision.

Not giving him the chance to change his mind, Francesca brought the car to a halt beneath the branches of an evergreen oak in the lane alongside the church.

Together they got out of the car, skirted the ivy-covered wall and made their way up the pathway between crumbling gravestones to the church porch. It was quiet in the still of the September afternoon, the only sounds the song of a blackbird from the top of a yew tree, the drone of a plane overhead and the faint hum of traffic from the village. The sun was still warm, so warm that the dim interior of the old stone church struck cold as they entered.

Francesca paused for a moment and gazed up the aisle to the chancel. The polished pews were empty now, the only flowers an arrangement of Michaelmas daisies and teasles in one of the stone window embrasures. The scent of lavender furniture polish hung in the air together with a trace of incense that lingered from the last service.

It was hard to believe that only two short weeks ago those same pews had been packed with family and friends, that the air had been filled with the fragrance of lilies, that the sound of Mendelssohn had reverberated round the old stone walls, and the man at her side had promised to spend the rest of his life with her.

And now. . . Francesca swallowed and stole a glance at Guy. He too was staring up the aisle towards the high altar.

What was he thinking? Was he remembering?

Even as she wondered, he turned, and when he found her watching him he said, 'Did you have bridesmaids?'

'No.' She paused and, when he didn't enlarge further, softly she asked, 'Why do you ask?'

'I just wondered, that's all. I didn't see any in the photos. . .' He trailed off, looking round the interior of the old church; at the stone pillars, the figures on the rood beam, the beautifully carved communion rail. But to Francesca, watching him, it was as if he were seeing them for the first time in his life.

'You don't remember any of it. . .?'

He shook his head. 'No, nothing. I wish I could,' he said desperately, 'I really wish I could.'

A clock in the tower above them suddenly chimed

the hour and as the sound of the strokes died away Francesca reached out and touched his arm. This time he didn't flinch, didn't pull away, didn't reject her.

'Don't worry,' she whispered, 'it may not all be for nothing. Something may be registering in your subconscious.'

'Yes, maybe.' He gave a rueful nod as if he didn't really believe it, then he lightly touched her fingers where they lay on his arm. Only then did he draw away from her and lead the way out of the church into the drowsy warmth of the afternoon sunshine.

He was very quiet for the rest of that day and Francesca wondered if it had all been a bit much for him; the morning at the centre, the wedding photos, the house calls and the visit to the church.

During supper she deliberately kept their conversation light; about the food they were eating, the view of the garden from the cottage and the music playing on the radio, anything rather than let Guy think she was still trying to jog his memory. But later, after she had showered and was preparing for bed, she found him once again going through their wedding photos.

He was sitting on the bed and she watched him from the open doorway of the bedroom.

'Guy,' she began at last, but he looked up quickly and spoke before she could continue.

'Do you still have this dress?' he asked and she couldn't fail to notice the sudden urgency in his voice.

'Of course. . .'

'I thought it might have been hired.'

'No,' she paused, 'it's in the wardrobe in the other room.'

'Would you put it on for me?'

She stared at him.

'Would you?' he repeated.

'Yes, of course.' She swallowed. 'Of course I will, Guy. If that's what you want. . .but don't you think you've had enough for one day——?'

'Please,' he interrupted, cutting her short.

'All right.' She nodded and slipped into the next

bedroom. She stood for one moment in front of the wardrobe, thinking, wondering. But something of Guy's sense of urgency had somehow transmitted itself to her and as her breath caught in her throat she tugged open the wardrobe door.

Her wedding outfit, the wild silk and champagne lace dress had been carefully wrapped in tissue, placed in a plastic cover and hung in the wardrobe by her mother after she and Guy had left for their honeymoon. Carefully, with trembling fingers, she slipped it out of its wrapping and draped it over the bed, then untied her bathrobe and let it slide to the floor.

She eased the garment over her head and as it slid down over her body the silk felt cool against her skin. Smoothing the material over her hips, she caught sight of her reflection in the full-length mirror inside the wardrobe door. Her dark hair was still damp from the shower but her cheeks were flushed, her eyes bright with excitement.

Taking a deep breath, she turned away from her reflection then, opening the door, stepped across the landing and pushed open the bedroom door.

CHAPTER EIGHT

She thought his breath caught in his throat when he saw her but she couldn't be sure.

'That perfume. . .' he said.

A faint trace of the scent Francesca had worn on her wedding-day still lingered in the folds of silk, and as she moved the warmth of her body released the elusive fragrance into the air.

Guy stared at her for a long time, a frown of concentration deepening on his forehead, then at last he stretched out his hand. 'Come here,' he said huskily.

Hardly daring to hope, she moved forward out of the doorway right into the room so that she stood before him.

Lightly he touched the silky material of the dress, his fingers brushing the softly rounded contour of her hip. 'You are so beautiful,' he murmured wonderingly.

For one wild moment she found herself believing he was remembering the last time he had seen her wearing the dress, the time he had gone on to remove it. She looked down, then tentatively she too reached out her hand, let it hover uncertainly over his bowed head, longing to touch him, to let her fingers sink into the thick fair hair, but at the same time still so afraid.

Then just when it seemed that once again he would lose the battle to clear the mists in his mind, Francesca sank to her knees beside him and, all reservation gone, put her arms around him and held him close. 'Oh, Guy,' she whispered, 'I love you so much.'

They remained close together for a long moment, then Francesca drew away from him, mindful of the warning not to rush him but at the same time having to battle with an overwhelming surge of desire. But, as she turned to go back to the spare room to take off her wedding-dress and replace it in its tissue wrapper, Guy rose abruptly to his feet and before she knew what was happening pulled her roughly into his arms. Heedless of the delicacy of the champagne lace, he crushed her against his chest and fiercely covered her mouth with his.

Aware that this might in some way be harmful, Francesca made a half-hearted attempt to struggle, then as his kiss grew more urgent she gave up and let herself enjoy the ecstasy of being in his arms again.

When at last he drew away he continued to hold her, his hands tightly gripping her arms while his eyes hungrily searched every inch of her face.

Then with a low moan he pulled her to him again. 'I want you,' he said. 'I'm sorry. I can't help it—but I want you.'

'Don't be sorry,' she whispered shakily. 'You are my husband.'

'Yes, but. . .'

'Shh.' Gently she placed her fingers over his lips to silence him. She could see the raw desire in his eyes, a need as urgent as her own, then, the last shred of restraint disappearing, for the second time he unfastened the zip of her wedding-dress and as it slid to the floor he lowered her on to the bed.

For a moment everything seemed unreal and Francesca found herself wondering if she was dreaming, if at any moment she might wake up, but the feel of Guy's hands on her body arousing and caressing her, the sound of his voice in her ear and the taste of his kisses on her tongue were all real enough. In the end she relaxed, stopped worrying about what Guy might or might not remember and gave herself up to the sheer joy of being loved by him again.

He took her in an agony of longing; her body remembered, and she could swear his did too. Their responses to each other were as instantaneous and utterly natural as those of animals that recognised their mate. Instinctively they found the pattern and rhythm they had so recently established for their loving and which had been so cruelly cut short. They soared together and afterwards, when he held her, although he was silent, Francesca detected an air of surprise about him as if he could not believe the depth of passion they had shared.

In the darkness she smiled, lying awake until Guy's breathing steadied and she knew he slept. She had no idea what the next day would bring but at that moment neither did she care, and eventually she too slept.

When she awoke she reached out her hand but Guy's side of the bed was empty. She listened but there was only silence in the cottage, and she stretched and lay for a while luxuriating in the memory of the night before. It had been every bit as wonderful as their honeymoon. Maybe at last, she thought happily, things would start to return to normal.

Eventually, when there was still no sound from downstairs, Francesca got out of bed and padded to the bathroom. She showered and dressed, still in a glow of happiness, then as she was halfway down the stairs Guy came through the front door.

'So there you are—well, good morning!' She stopped and smiled, one hand on the banister, while Guy paused in the tiny hallway and looked up at her.

'I went for a walk,' he said abruptly.

'You should have woken me,' she replied, 'I would have come with you.'

He didn't reply, instead disappearing into the kitchen without even another glance in her direction. Puzzled, she followed him and found him starting to make breakfast.

She watched him for a while as he made toast and she was just on the point of making some light-hearted remark about the night before when something stopped her, something in his manner urging caution, making her question whether he even remembered what had happened.

The possibility that he hadn't was frightening, because it would mean he had suffered another, second lapse. If that was the case it was something that would have to be faced, but somehow she couldn't bring herself to do so.

Not yet, when the memory was still so fresh in her own mind, when it was all still so wonderful. . .

No, for the moment at least, she was content to leave things as they were and just let events take their natural course.

Their lives for the next week followed a similar pattern to that first day back at work. They continued to go into the clinic each morning, where Francesca would take surgery and Guy would carry on with his reading and his catching up with medical events during the past eighteen months. They would lunch together, then more often than not Guy would accompany her on her house calls. But there the similarity to that first day ended, for he made no further attempt to make love to her. Still she couldn't bring herself to ask him if he recalled having done so for fear that either he didn't or, and the possibility was somehow even worse, that, having attempted it once, he had no desire to repeat the experience. The prospect of the latter appalled her so much that she hardly dared contemplate what she would do if it proved to be true.

Guy himself seemed to quickly re-adapt to life at the surgery and while accompanying Francesca on house calls soon familiarised himself with the locality and the residents. In the end it was hard to believe there was anything wrong with him.

'I can't see any reason why you shouldn't start taking surgery again soon,' said David during a staff meeting at the beginning of the second week.

'How do you feel about that, Guy?' Malcolm looked up from a sheaf of letters he had been signing.

'I feel quite competent.' Guy had been leaning back in his chair, toying with a pen on the table before him. He glanced round at the others then sat up straight.

'In that case——' David began, but Guy cut him short.

'Hang on a minute, David,' he said. 'I appreciate the faith you all have in me, but the fact remains that, in spite of everyone's efforts, my memory still hasn't returned. In fairness to you all,' he glanced round the table, 'I've decided that before I return to work officially I'm going to go to a chap I know at a hospital in Carlisle for a complete check-up.'

'I can't see that's necessary.' David too glanced round at the others, who murmured their agreement, and Francesca found herself wondering for the umpteenth time whether Guy had suffered a second memory lapse and forgotten that he had made love to her.

'It's necessary to me,' said Guy quietly.

'Very well.' It was Malcolm who replied. 'In that case you must do it. Do you want one of us to give you a referral?'

Guy shook his head. 'No, thanks, I've already made an appointment.'

'You didn't tell me,' said Francesca when they were alone later, trying not to sound accusing.

'No,' he agreed. 'I didn't. There are some things I have to come to terms with and sort out for myself.'

'Fair enough.' She shrugged, then suddenly on a wild impulse she said, 'Like when you made love to me the other night?'

It was after their evening meal and they were still sitting at the table, the coffee-pot between them. She was watching him carefully and she saw him stiffen.

'Maybe,' he said without looking at her.

'You remember it?' she asked and found she was holding her breath as she waited for his reply.

'Of course.' He paused, then glanced up at her. 'Didn't you think I would?'

'I didn't know what to think.' Leaning forward across the table, she poured herself more coffee.

'You thought I'd suffered another memory lapse?' he asked quietly.

'Like I said, I didn't know what to think.' She hesitated, then when he remained silent she went on, 'You made no mention of it. . .yet neither has it happened again.'

'Maybe you were expecting an apology?' There was a raw edge to his voice now.

'An apology?' She stared at him. 'Why should I want an apology? You're my husband, for God's sake!'

'Exactly,' he said tightly.

'I don't understand.' She set her cup down in the saucer with a clatter. 'What do you mean?'

'What do I mean?' he mused, staring at the floor. 'Well, for you,' he raised his head then and looked at her, 'it wasn't any different—or maybe it was; I wouldn't know. . .at least you had something to compare with.'

'I still don't understand what you're driving at.' She tried to remain calm but was finding it increasingly difficult. 'Are you trying to tell me it was awful, that you didn't enjoy it? Is that it? Is that what you're saying, Guy?' She was aware that her voice was becoming shrill but was powerless to stop it. 'Because if that's it then you'd better come right out and say so——'

'You know that's not it,' he said roughly, staring into his cup.

'I don't know anything of the sort,' she began frantically, 'in fact, I doubt I know anything any more——'

'It was fantastic,' he muttered. 'Bloody fantastic and you know it was!'

She stared at him, her mouth open. 'Then what. . .?' she cried in anguish. 'You've lost me, Guy.' When he didn't answer she went on in exasperation, 'You say you do remember it and that it was fantastic, but you haven't bothered to mention it when you know I'm doing everything in my power to try to get things back to normal as quickly as I can. Neither do you seem particularly keen to repeat the experience—so what the hell am I supposed to think?'

'Have you ever made love with a stranger?' he asked suddenly without looking up.

'What. . .?'

'With someone you hardly know. . .?' He did look up then, his level grey gaze meeting hers.

'You mean a one-night stand?' She frowned.

'If you like.' He shrugged. 'Yes.'

'Definitely not.'

'Well, that's what that was like for me,' he said softly.

She stared at him in exasperation. 'I don't see how it can be,' she cried at last, running both hands through her hair in distraction, hating the comparison he was making. 'We're married, for heaven's sake!'

'*You* know we're married,' he said quietly, '*I* know we're married, but only because you told me so and because I've seen photographs of us that show we were married. I don't remember marrying you, I don't remember making love to you before the other night. As far as I'm concerned I've only known you about a week.' He stood up abruptly, his chair screeching on the stone floor.

She stared up at him, her frustration growing. 'But if I'm prepared to accept that. . .!'

'I feel as if I'm using you, damn it!' he shouted, bringing his clenched fists down on to the table with such force that the coffee-cups rattled in their saucers. 'Can't you see that? I wanted you. . .wanted you like hell. . .but is that all it was. . .lust?'

Helplessly they stared at each other until Guy lowered his head in despair.

'Oh, God, I'm sorry,' he groaned. 'Please try to understand.'

'Oh, Guy,' she whispered, her eyes filling with hot tears. 'I do, I do, really I do. . .it's just that I love you. . .and all this is tearing me apart.'

He straightened up and walked to the window,

where he stood for a time, obviously struggling to get his emotions under control, then at last he turned to her. 'Maybe we've handled this all wrong,' he said quietly.

'What do you mean?'

'Perhaps we should just concentrate on getting to know each other again...the way we obviously must have done before. Maybe we will fall in love all over again.'

'David said that,' she said slowly.

'David?' He turned sharply. 'What's he got to do with any of this?'

'Nothing.' She stared at him, her exasperation rising again at his apparent unreasonableness. 'David has nothing to do with anything, honestly.' She paused. 'Why are you so touchy about him? He's your friend, for heaven's sake!'

He shook his head. 'I don't know what it is... there's something about David that's irritating me but I can't remember what it is.' He hesitated, then he said, 'Was I jealous of him?'

'Jealous?'

'Yes, did I have cause to be jealous?'

'No, of course not.' She paused, considering, wondering what she should say. 'There was a joke,' she said slowly at last, 'but it was nothing...'

'What joke?' he asked quickly.

'Between you and David. Something left over from your medical-school days, I should imagine. Something about which one of you gets the girl.' He stared at her in silence. 'Do you remember that?' she asked.

He nodded. 'Yes, of course, I remember all that from medical school...but I don't see what that has to do with our relationship...unless...unless you were David's girl before you were mine.'

Francesca remained silent, struggling to find the right words, aware that whatever she said could be misconstrued in this abnormal situation.

'Were you?' he asked at last and there was a rough edge to his voice. 'Were you David's girl?'

'Not exactly.'

'What do you mean, not exactly? Either you were or you weren't.'

'Guy!' she cried. 'How far do you intend taking this interrogation?'

He continued to face her, a scowl on his handsome features, then his shoulders dropped and he turned away. 'Sorry,' he muttered, 'I had no right.'

'No,' she agreed, 'you didn't. But if it makes any difference, David and I were friends—still are, for that matter—and yes, at one time David wanted more.'

'And you?'

She shook her head. 'No, I always knew David wasn't right for me. When you came on the scene David was away, when he returned you and I were on the point of marrying—there was a lot of good-natured gibing from David about knowing he shouldn't have left me with you around, that sort of thing—and that, Guy, is all there was to it. In fact, it bothered you so little that David was your natural choice for best man. You'd hardly have wanted that if there was any bitterness between you. . .would you?'

'No, I suppose not,' he muttered. 'It's just that I felt there was something. . .something concerning David that was bothering me and I don't know what it was. . .'

'Have you tried mentioning this to David?'

'Sort of. . .'

'And what was his reaction?'

'I don't think he had a clue what I was talking about.'

'Well, there you are. I'm sure there isn't anything, Guy, and there certainly isn't anything concerning David and me. Please take my word for it.'

As Francesca finished speaking one of Percy's chrysanthemums, which she had placed in a pottery jug on the dresser, suddenly shed its petals over the polished oak surface. The movement, slight as it was, caught the attention of them both and they watched the flowers as if expecting the others to follow suit.

When it became evident that the remaining blooms

had no intention of doing anything dramatic, Guy said, 'Didn't we discuss previous relationships before we... before we married?'

'We did.' Francesca nodded. 'Of course we did.'

'And did you mention David?'

'Not in that context, no.' She took a deep breath, wishing this bizarre conversation didn't have to happen. 'It simply wasn't relevant,' she added.

She got to her feet, moved to the dresser and picked up the copper-coloured petals, holding them in the palm of her hand. 'Neil,' she said at last, 'yes, but not David.'

Guy's head jerked up. 'Neil? Who the hell is Neil?'

Coolly Francesca raised her eyebrows. 'Neil *was* a previous boyfriend.'

'It was serious?' His eyes narrowed and Francesca found herself rolling the petals into a tight little ball.

'Yes, Guy, it was serious,' she admitted, 'at least, at the time it was.'

'I see,' he said tightly and she was amazed to see that suddenly he looked miserable.

She watched him affectionately for a moment then laughed. 'Oh, come on, Guy, be reasonable, did you really think I'd got to thirty-two without forming any relationships?'

'No, I suppose not,' he muttered. 'So what happened—to this Neil?'

'What do you mean, what happened?' Francesca smiled. She was beginning to enjoy herself.

'Well, who was he, for a start?'

'Do you know, Guy, if I didn't know better I would say you were jealous.' She said it light-heartedly but Guy remained serious. 'He was a registrar at the hospital where I was an SHO,' she concluded.

'And?'

'We were together for a couple of years.'

'As long as that?' She nodded. 'So why did it end?' he asked after a moment.

'The relationship wasn't going anywhere.'

'And you thought it should?'

She glanced away from him, aware he was watching her closely. 'Yes, I happen to think if a relationship doesn't progress it dies.'

'Which is what happened in this case?'

'Exactly,' she replied firmly. 'It wasn't going anywhere and it died.'

He was silent for a moment and she thought he was going to let the matter rest; then he said, 'But you wanted it to go somewhere?'

She shrugged. 'At the time I did; now I'm glad it didn't. As far as I'm concerned that particular relationship is well and truly dead and buried.' She paused and looked up, allowing her gaze to meet his again. 'Does that answer your questions?'

'Yes. . .' he hesitated then threw her a quick, almost sheepish glance '. . .yes, it does. . .' He paused. 'Was I sounding like an interrogator?'

'Just a bit.' She pulled a face.

'Sorry,' he muttered. 'I just find it hard not knowing. . .not being able to remember what you told me and what you didn't tell me. . .and then when I learn of other people in your life. . .I just wonder, that's all. . .'

'I feel a bit like that about Chloe,' she said quietly.

The moment she'd said it she wished she hadn't. No undue pressure, the others had said. She looked up quickly to see his reaction and saw he had grown very still.

'Chloe?' he said at last without looking at her. 'What do you know about Chloe?'

'Not a lot,' she admitted. 'I was waiting for you to tell me.'

'Did I tell you about her before. . .before the accident?'

'No.'

'Then how did you know. . .?' He looked up then and at the bewilderment in his eyes Francesca again wished she'd never mentioned the woman, whoever she was.

'It was when we were in the hospital in Spain,' she

said reluctantly. 'Helen Ryder had just told you she had brought your wife to see you, and before you looked up and saw me you assumed I was someone called Chloe.'

He continued to stare at her.

Francesca remained silent for a while, her heart thudding, then softly she said, 'So who is she, Guy? Who is Chloe? Or can't you remember that either?'

'Oh, yes,' he said quietly at last. 'I can remember Chloe. I think it would take more than amnesia to forget Chloe.'

'In that case,' Francesca swallowed, 'she obviously made a greater impression on you than I did.'

'No,' he shook his head, 'I didn't mean that—it's just that Chloe has a rather overwhelming personality.'

'And you thought you'd married her?'

'For a moment there—yes, I did,' he admitted. 'Or rather it was more that I feared I might have married her.'

'But why, why should you think that? She must have meant a lot to you at one time.' When he didn't answer she said, 'So who was she?'

'Chloe,' he said slowly, 'was a secretary at the hospital where I was working in the States. I dated her, or rather I was dating her. . .and that's all I can remember. . . As I told you before, my memory seems to stop around that time. . .'

'Had marriage been mentioned between you?' She was curious now but it was as if they were discussing someone else and not Guy.

'I don't know. . .' He shook his head as if trying to clear the mists. 'I really don't know. . .I guess it must have been if I thought. . .if I thought you were Chloe. . . Oh, God, I really don't know. . .this is awful, Francesca, it really is. . .'

She laughed then at his horrified expression. 'Come on,' she said, 'cheer up, it can't be that bad.'

His expression cleared a little but he continued to look doubtful, and later, when she was alone, Francesca couldn't help but wonder anew about the mysterious Chloe, the American girl whose personality had made such an impression on Guy that he thought the relationship might have been leading to marriage.

CHAPTER NINE

IT WAS one of those glorious days of early autumn when the deep cobalt-blue of the sky was reflected in the lakes, and the gold of the leaves had already started to take on a deeper, richer tone, preparing for the russets and copper to come.

Francesca had managed to change her day off with David so that she was free to drive Guy to Carlisle for his check-up. He hadn't driven since his accident, preferring to wait until he had discussed it with the consultant he had arranged to see.

Because it was such a beautiful day and because they had plenty of time she took the route over the fells, intending to pick up the M6 motorway at Penrith. Guy was very quiet as they drove and she knew he was apprehensive over the outcome of his appointment.

The week since their argument about past relationships had been a strange mixture of lulls interpersed with sudden outbursts when Guy would demand to know something, often accusing Francesca of deliberately keeping things from him. Usually after these outbursts or mood swings he was sorry and, although Francesca always forgave him, each episode left her feeling drained.

In spite of this she felt they were gradually beginning to build a new relationship, somewhat different from their first, a relationship where Guy relied on her, depending on her to be there when he needed her, to rescue him from awkward situations.

'I feel,' he said once, 'how a blind man must when he relies on someone to be his eyes—only in my case I feel as if you've become my soul.'

He'd said it in a faintly rueful fashion, but when Francesca, overcome by his words, had reached out and silently gripped his hands, he too had seemed overwhelmed by what was happening to them.

Now as she sat beside him in her car Francesca stole a glance in his direction. His face was half turned away from her and he appeared to be studying the landscape below them. She was about to speak, to ask if he was all right, when she realised he was leaning forward slightly, staring at something almost out of their vision below a dip in the hills.

Taking her eyes briefly from the road, she craned her neck to see what he was looking at. Then as the roof and chimneypots of Sky Fell Farm came into sight she threw another quick look at Guy. He was frowning now, his expression intent.

'What is it, Guy?' she asked, trying to keep her voice casual.

'That place,' he said slowly. 'What is it?'

'That's Sky Fell Farm,' she replied.

'Do I know it? Have I been there?'

'Yes,' she said quietly. 'Do you remember something?'

'No.' He shook his head and her heart sank. Just for one moment she thought he might be remembering their first meeting.

'No,' he said again as they passed the farm and the road dipped down, 'I don't remember it. . .but do you know. . .back there. . .the most extraordinary thing. . .?'

'What, Guy?' she asked.

'No.' He shook his head again. 'It's too ridiculous for words. . .on such a glorious day as this. . .it couldn't possibly be. . .'

'Tell me,' she insisted.

'It was back there——' he looked over his shoulder '—as we passed that farm. . .just for a moment. . .I could have sworn it was snowing. . .'

'You must tell him that,' Francesca said later as she pulled on to the hospital car park in Carlisle and switched off the engine.

Guy sat very still, making no attempt to get out of

the car. 'You think it was significant?' he said at last.

'Definitely,' replied Francesca. 'Another glimpse behind the curtain.'

'What do you mean...another glimpse?' he said wryly. 'I don't recall too many others.'

'But there have been others!' she said urgently. 'There have, Guy...you knew it was a red car that caused our accident...'

'That could have been pure speculation...'

'I don't think it was...but there have been other things...little things, probably insignificant to anyone else...but to me...

She shrugged, then when Guy continued to look sceptical in desperation she went on, 'There was one morning at the surgery when I handed you a mug of coffee and you spoke of a strong sense of *déjà vu*...that was something, I swear it was...'

'Lots of people experience *déjà vu*...'

'I know, but in your case I'm sure it was a start...'

'I think you're being overly optimistic,' he said, then when she remained silent, he said abruptly, 'Well, I suppose I'd better get this over with; at least he may be able to tell me if I'm fit to work again.'

She watched him as he got out of the car, not daring to offer to go with him, afraid of a rebuff, a reminder that this was something he had to do for himself.

Taking his jacket from the rear seat of the car, he straightened up, slipped it on then adjusted his tie. She thought he was about to move away when suddenly he bent down and looked into the car again.

'Come with me,' he said.

Pleasure washed over her. 'Of course,' she said and took the keys from the ignition.

'Well, at least you can get on with your life now.' Malcolm Westray bit into a cheese and lettuce roll. It was the day after Guy's appointment and the partners and Ros were gathering for a lunchtime meeting.

'I missed that—what did you say?' David, who had

just come into the room, crossed to the table and poured himself a coffee.

'We were talking about Guy's appointment with Robert Carstairs,' said Malcolm. 'He's given Guy a clean bill of health.'

'I'm glad to hear it,' said David in mock-relief. 'I was getting sick to death of him skiving around the place—it's about time he got back to work.' He grinned at Guy as he spoke. 'Not that it comes as any surprise,' he added, 'I never had any doubts that Guy was capable of practising again.'

'I needed to be sure,' said Guy quietly. 'It's people's lives we're talking about here.'

'I know.' David grew serious again. 'So are you sure now?'

Francesca found herself watching Guy, waiting for his answer.

'Yes, I think so,' he said at last. 'Robert convinced me that I haven't lost anything crucial to my training, at least nothing that can't be caught up on, and I believe I've almost done that. He also doesn't think there should be any further memory lapse now.'

'But what about the chunk you lost? Will you get that back?' It was Ros who put into words what the others were undoubtedly thinking.

'He couldn't say for sure.' Guy shrugged. 'He asked me a lot of questions and from what I told him he seemed to think I would gradually recall what is missing, but on the other hand it may never come back and if that's the case I shall just have to learn to live with it.'

'Thank God it wasn't a longer period of time,' said Ros.

'That's true,' replied Malcolm, reaching out for a second cheese roll, hesitating, no doubt mindful of his ulcer, then taking it anyway. 'As it is, I think you might have got away with no one finding out. . .where people here didn't know you before anyway. . .' He left the sentence unfinished and continued with his lunch.

'So when will you start surgeries again?' asked David.

'As soon as you like.'

'How about this afternoon?' asked Ros jokingly.

'Hey, steady on,' protested Francesca.

'Sorry. It's just that I'm at my wits' end trying to cope with all the appointments,' replied Ros with a sheepish grin.

'This afternoon is fine,' said Guy, standing up. 'No time like the present and David is quite right, it is high time I stopped skiving.'

'Well, you won't get any objections from me,' said Malcolm. 'I'm on call and the list of extra patients is threatening to get the better of me.'

'Do you feel ready to face the public?' asked Francesca anxiously.

Guy shrugged. 'As ready as I'll ever be—I'll probably upset a few people because I don't remember things about them that they consider I should, but what the hell. . .?'

'I shouldn't let that worry you,' mumbled Malcolm. 'That happens to me all the time.'

Francesca was sorting through some records with Marie at the reception desk at the end of afternoon surgery when Guy strolled out of his consulting-room.

'How did it go?' she asked anxiously.

'Fine,' he replied easily. 'No problem. Just one more to see. Ah, Mrs Walsh,' he said, glancing at the appointment book, then, moving to the doorway of the waiting-room, he called, 'Alice!'

Mrs Walsh, looking pink and flustered at being called by her Christian name in front of the other patients, limped out of the waiting-room and smiled up at Guy, who said, 'Come on, Alice.' Just before they disappeared into his room Guy turned, one hand on the door handle, and winked at Francesca and Marie.

Francesca shook her head and Marie chuckled. 'He's a natural with the old folk, they love him, and do you know what I think?' she said, lowering her voice so that no one else could hear. 'I think he's having us all on. I don't think he's lost his memory at all.'

'Now there's a thought. . .' Francesca left the sentence unfinished and they looked at each other.

'Ooh,' breathed Marie, 'that's a bit spooky, isn't it?'

'Definitely,' replied Francesca with a laugh.

They continued checking records for a while then Malcolm came out of his room and Francesca noticed he looked less harassed than he had earlier.

'I've just had a call from the hospital,' he said. 'Lauren Richardson is being discharged in a couple of days' time.'

'Oh, that's good,' said Marie. 'Poor little mite.'

'Has she been in hospital ever since she came back from Florida?' asked Francesca.

Malcolm nodded. 'Yes, she was very poorly after the return flight—she's had to have more chemotherapy.'

'Let's hope the trip was worth it,' Francesca mused.

'According to Mrs Richardson it was,' said Malcolm. 'Apparently Lauren had a wonderful time and doesn't stop talking about it.'

'Ah, well, that's good.' Francesca glanced up as Guy's door opened again and he reappeared, accompanying Alice Walsh. His head was bent to her level and he seemed to be in deep conversation with the old lady.

As they reached the desk Guy looked up and, catching sight of Francesca, he said, 'Have you finished surgery?' When she nodded in reply, he said, 'Good, we can take Alice home in that case—save her calling a taxi.'

Guy escorted Alice to the car and by the time Francesca took her place behind the wheel the old lady was happily ensconced in the rear seat.

'I hear your husband is to have his own list of patients,' she said, raising her voice above the sound of the engine so that Francesca and Guy could hear.

'Yes, that's the general idea,' Francesca called over her shoulder.

'Who will he have?' asked Alice.

'Well, for a start any new people who come into the area,' replied Francesca.

Alice was quiet for a moment, then she said, 'I know I'm registered with Dr Elcombe. . .' Francesca and Guy exchanged a swift glance, anticipating what was coming. 'But do you think I would be able to change. . .? Do you think Dr Elcombe would be upset?'

'I shouldn't think so, Alice,' replied Francesca, then, unable to resist it, she added, 'He and Dr Sinclair are used to a certain amount of competition.' She shot another swift glance in Guy's direction and he raised his eyebrows at her.

'Oh, I've nothing against Dr Elcombe,' said Alice quickly, 'he's a very nice young man, but I haven't really seen much of him. . .I was so used to your father, Francesca, and it's hard at my age to get used to change. . .'

'But you won't mind changing to Dr Sinclair?'

'Oh, no,' said Alice. 'He understands me, he's never in a hurry and well, quite honestly, Francesca, he reminds me of your father in so many ways, especially when he treats my leg. . .he is so gentle.'

'Maybe that's what you saw in me as well,' muttered Guy out of the side of his mouth, so quietly that only Francesca heard, 'that I reminded you of your father.'

There was little chance for further conversation as Alice proceeded to talk non-stop, covering every subject from her family and her hospital appointments to her cat. She had just started on the National Health Service when they arrived at the cottages. Guy helped her out of the car and accompanied her inside.

While Francesca was locking the car two other cars drew up behind hers and stopped. Two men got out of the cars and approached Francesca; one was dressed in a pinstriped suit, the other in dark blue overalls and a red baseball cap.

'Dr Sinclair.' The man in the suit grinned and dangled a set of keys in the air. 'One Rover saloon. Is your husband around?'

'Oh, yes.' Francesca glanced over her shoulder but Guy had disappeared inside Alice's cottage. 'Give me the keys,' she said quickly. 'It'll be a surprise for him.'

Seconds later Francesca tapped on Alice's open front door and called out to Guy, who was still inside.

He appeared in the tiny hallway. 'What is it?' he said. 'I've just been putting the kettle on for Alice. . .' He trailed off as he caught sight of her expression.' 'Francesca?' She didn't speak, simply holding up the keys and dangling them in the air as the salesman had done. 'What. . .?' He frowned then looked beyond her, past the front gardens of the cottages to the road beyond. 'Oh, I say. . .you mean. . .?' He threw her another glance and when she nodded his face lit up with sudden pleasure. 'My new car. . .?'

'Come and see,' she said, then added, 'Have a look at what you chose.' She turned from the door and he followed her down the short garden path.

The salesman and the mechanic were just about to drive away in their own car. They both grinned and nodded as they caught sight of Guy, and the mechanic gave a thumbs-up sign. Francesca smiled back, then as they drove away she turned to Guy to see his reaction.

He was standing very still, one hand on Alice's gate as he gazed at his new Rover.

She remained silent for a moment, then when he still made no comment she said anxiously, 'Do you like it?'

'Did I choose that colour?' he asked slowly.

'Yes,' she said quietly, 'you particularly wanted red.'

'I see.' He let go of the gate and slowly walked towards the car.

Francesca watched him. 'Does it bother you?' she asked at last as he walked round the car, touching it, inspecting it.

He looked at her then across the bonnet. 'No,' he said, 'of course not. Why should it?'

'I don't know.' She shrugged. 'I just wondered if it would. . .' She paused, hesitating. 'It didn't stir any memory when you first saw it?'

'No, I don't think it did.' He shook his head and opened the door, looking into the interior, at the dashboard and the soft leather seats. 'Had you hoped it might?' he said, looking up again before he got inside.

'I don't know.' She shrugged again, helplessly this time. 'I suppose I just thought it might.'

He stared thoughtfully at her for a moment. 'Coming for a spin?' he said at last and his tone had softened, as if he'd found it touching that she had been living in hope that the arrival of his new car might have been significant in restoring his memory.

'You're going to drive?'

'Carstairs didn't see any reason why I shouldn't.'

'In that case...what are we waiting for?' Shutting Alice's gate behind her, Francesca opened the car door and slid into the passenger-seat.

Guy started the engine and they drew away from the kerb. 'Where to?' he asked.

She hesitated for only a moment. 'Turn left at the end of the road,' she said, 'and I'll direct you from there.'

They drove for several miles, out of Bletchley Bridge into Windermere, along the side of the lake past the hotel where they'd held their wedding reception and into Ambleside, then on through the village of Hawkshead. Eventually, on Francesca's instructions, Guy pulled off the road on to a single track and about a mile further on he brought the car to a halt.

For a long time they sat in silence, looking down at the still green waters of the lake below them.

'Which one is this?' asked Guy at last. 'I've got the bigger ones sorted out now—Windermere and Coniston, even Grasmere and Rydal Water—but this one...?'

'This is Tarn Hows,' she said softly. 'My favourite of all.'

'Is that so...?' He fell silent again and they stared down at the curling bracken that fringed the water, the gold of the trees on the far banks, the rich green of a band of conifers in the distance and the deep purple of the heather on the slopes beyond.

But in spite of the majestic beauty of the scene Francesca's heart remained heavy, for she knew he hadn't remembered that it had been here that he had told her he was in love with her. It had been a long shot in guiding him here, and she hadn't held out too many hopes as to the outcome, but it had been worth a try.

'Are you pleased with the car?' she said, breaking the silence at last and running her hand over the dashboard.

'Yes,' he nodded. 'She runs like a dream.'

She hesitated, then said, 'I took a chance not telling you about the colour.'

'What do you mean?' He leaned back in his seat and half turned towards her.

'Well, I suppose I was gambling on the fact that it was possible. . .because you might have remembered the colour of the other car in the accident, and because this was the same. . .I thought. . .I thought. . . Oh, I don't know what I thought really.' She stared at him helplessly as the improbability of the idea finally hit her. 'It could easily have been harmful, I suppose, making you try to recall the trauma itself. . . Oh, I don't know. . .I'm not sure why I did it. . .' She trailed off and turned her head away from him, staring out of the window at the lake below.

'I know why you did it,' he said, his voice breaking into her jumbled thoughts.

'What?' She would have turned, but she felt his hand beneath her jaw as if he was about to turn her face towards him. She froze, unable to move, then he released her jaw and brushed the backs of his fingers tenderly down the side of her cheek.

'You did it,' he said softly, 'because you love me and because you won't give up in your quest to help me regain my memory. You want me to remember that I love you, don't you?'

'Of course I do.' She turned to him then, her

eyes full of pain. 'Is that so unbelievable?'

'No, not unbelievable.' Leaning forward, he took her face between both his hands, his thumbs beneath her jaw, his fingers entangled in the dark unruly mass of her hair. 'Not unbelievable,' he repeated, gazing deeply into her eyes, 'but more and more unnecessary with every day that passes.'

'What do you mean?' She stared back into the cool grey eyes, feeling as if she was drowning in their depths but at the same time quite content to do so.

'What do I mean?' he murmured. 'I mean quite simply that with each day that passes I understand more and more why I fell in love you, why I married you.' Moving his thumbs, he tilted her face. 'What I still don't understand,' he murmured, his voice husky with emotion, 'is why you married me.'

'Oh, Guy,' she whispered, then as his lips closed over hers she gave up all attempts at reasoning or explaining.

His kiss was long and lingering, stirring her desires, awakening the passion that for so long now had seethed under the surface, unfulfilled.

When at last he drew away from her he looked shaken as if he too was deeply moved.

'Let's walk for a while,' he muttered at last and his voice had an edge to it, an edge difficult to define, possibly one of frustration; almost certainly of excitement.

She nodded, not trusting her voice, and scrambled from the car, waiting amid the ferns while he locked the car before joining her.

The last rays from the sun as it slipped slowly behind a distant peak lightened the waters of the lake below them while a soft evening breeze ruffled the calm surface.

Leaving the car, they picked a pathway through the bracken and as Guy took her hand Francesca felt like a teenager on her first date. They walked for about half a mile through the full burnished glory of the autumn evening, only stopping when they left the pathway and entered the coolness of a coppice of silver birch and sycamores.

Once again Guy drew her into his arms and gazed down at her.

'I still can't believe my luck,' he said softly, holding her close. 'This feeling of unreality is probably because this whole thing is a dream. I think I'd better make the most of it before I wake up and find you aren't real.'

'Well, if it is a dream,' she smiled, 'then I'm in it as well—so why don't we both enjoy it?'

He kissed her again, a kiss of deep exploration, then, pulling away, he led her beneath the silvery leaves of the birches and gently drew her down beside him, gathering her into his arms.

He made love to her there, in that silent, secret place above Tarn Hows, the place where he had first told her he loved her. This time his lovemaking had none of the desperation of the last time; this time it was easy, unhurried, an awakening of the senses; the smell of him mingled with the scent of the bracken, the sight of his face above hers and the expression of love in his eyes, the taste of his kisses on her lips, the feel of his skin against hers and the touch of his hands, teasing and caressing.

And this time, as he moved inside her in the sweet rhythm of their love and reached the peak of his pleasure, he called her name, as he had used to do, and then, at last, once more he told her he loved her.

With her eyes closed, reluctant to break the spell, she held him, and for a long time he lay beside her, his body warm against hers.

When eventually the soft chill of a breeze rippled through the bracken and she moved, opening her eyes, it was to find him propped on one elbow, chewing a blade of grass and watching her.

'Hi,' he said softly.

'Hi yourself.' She smiled, a lazy, contented smile.

'Sorry about the unconventional venue.' He grinned, tracing the piece of grass down the length of her nose and around her lips.

'Don't be.' She wrinkled her nose as the grass tickled and a sneeze threatened. 'I'm well used to it.'

He stared at her. 'You are?'

'Oh, yes,' she replied airily, amused by his slightly shocked expression. 'All the time.'

'You mean, we...here?' He glanced over his shoulder in sudden awe as if the area had suddenly taken on a whole new meaning.

She laughed then, the sound echoing in the stillness. 'No, not here,' she said, 'but just about everywhere else...'

His eyes widened. 'Tell me more...I'm intrigued...'

'Well, let me see, now...' she paused, pretending to consider '...there was the time in Spain on the beach under the stars...'

'Really?' He sat up straight but continued to stare down at her.

'Oh, yes, and by the pool...'

'By the pool...?'

'And in the pool...!'

'In the pool?' He was laughing now.

'Yes, and under the pines on a Spanish mountainside...and in just about every room in the villa. Wait, no, I tell a lie, not the kitchen...we didn't get to the kitchen...but maybe that's just as well—marble tiles and worktops can't be too comfortable...'

'Oh, I don't know,' he mused thoughtfully, chewing his piece of grass again. 'It would be different... maybe we should try it some time.'

'Guy Sinclair—you're impossible!' She threw him a light punch and when he laughed and caught her wrist she pulled him down on to her again.

Twilight was deepening into dusk when much, much later, their arms entwined, they strolled back to the car.

Bletchley Bridge was almost deserted when they drove through, but as they passed the row of stone houses beside the church a figure in one of the gardens paused to stare then raised an arm in an uncertain wave as if dubious of the identity of the occupants of the car.

'Wasn't that Ros?' asked Guy, throwing Francesca a questioning look.

'Yes,' she replied. 'I don't think she was sure whether it was us or not in this car.'

'Does she live alone?' asked Guy after a moment as they left the town behind and approached the bridge.

'No, with her mother,' replied Francesca.

Guy was silent for a moment then with an unexpectedness that took her breath away he said, 'I wish she and David would get together; it's not as if either of them is getting any younger.'

For one moment she wondered if she'd misheard and, suddenly speechless, she found herself waiting for Guy to elaborate further. When he didn't she threw him a sidelong glance, but he was staring ahead, concentrating on the road.

'What do you mean, Guy,' she asked at last, 'about Ros and David?'

'Well, she is in love with him.' He said it in a matter-of-fact way.

'Is she?' Francesca asked quietly.

'Well, isn't she?' He was frowning. In spite of the gathering gloom, she could tell he was frowning.

'I don't know. You tell me.' She paused and when the silence became almost unbearable she said curiously, 'What makes you think she is?'

'I don't know,' he said and gave his head a shake as if to clear his brain. 'But it's obvious, isn't it?'

'No. . .' She shook her head. 'At least, not to me it isn't. . .and I don't think anyone else is aware of it either,' she added.

While they had been talking they had reached the cottage and as Guy brought the car to a halt they sat in silence, making no attempt to get out.

'How did you reach this conclusion, Guy?' she turned her head and looked at him.

'I don't know.' He shook his head again, in bewilderment this time. 'I was just aware of it, that's all...I don't know whether it's intuition from observing Ros when David's around or what it is...but you watch her, Francesca, and you'll see that I'm right.'

'But is David aware of how she feels?' She frowned, growing increasingly uneasy that she could have missed this between two people she thought she knew so well.

'Ah, that I don't know. Maybe he is but doesn't feel the same way...or maybe he's afraid it would be on the rebound from you...'

'Guy,' she took a deep breath, suddenly alarmed that something was about to spoil their newly found closeness, 'I told you, David never meant anything to me in that way.'

'Ah,' he said softly and lightly touched her cheek, 'I know you did, and I believe you, and maybe to you it didn't mean anything, but can you be sure it meant nothing to David?' As he finished speaking he suddenly leaned across the passenger-seat and kissed the tip of her nose. 'Come on, Mrs Sinclair,' he said, 'it's way past my suppertime.'

'Very well.' She sighed and opened her door. 'And what does the doctor order for his supper?'

'He's not really bothered,' replied Guy, then with a chuckle he added, 'Provided he gets an early night afterwards.' He paused. 'You know something?' Francesca glanced back over her shoulder at him and he said, 'I think this falling in love all over again is a very good idea—in fact, I could get to like it.'

CHAPTER TEN

FOR the next few days Francesca found herself watching Ros, especially when David was around, but there was nothing in the other woman's behaviour or body language to even hint that her feelings for her employer were anything other than platonic.

'Are you sure you aren't imagining it?' she asked Guy one morning when she slipped into his consulting-room before surgery.

'Positive,' he replied.' You just wait and see.'

Shaking her head, Francesca returned to her room. If it was true that Ros was eating her heart out and David was either oblivious to the fact or unable to reciprocate, Francesca felt sorry for her. But at the same time she herself had been so happy for the past few days that she was finding it difficult enough as it was to concentrate on her work without looking for added anxieties. Because, while Guy seemed no closer to recovering his memory, the impossible appeared to be happening, as he really did seem to be falling in love with her all over again.

In a determined attempt to concentrate, Francesca began looking through her morning mail and the inevitable pile of daily medical-test results. One result in particular caught her eye and she studied the laboratory findings with care, then, picking up her phone, she asked the receptionist to give her an outside line.

Jean Blake herself answered the call.

'Hello, Jean, it's Dr Sinclair,' Francesca said, endeavouring to sound as casual as possible.

'Oh, good morning, Doctor. . .'

'Jean, I have the result of your smear test here.'

'Oh, I was going to ring up for that.' Jean paused, then said, 'There's nothing wrong, is there?'

Francesca immediately detected the anxiety in her voice as Jean inevitably began to wonder why her doctor had rung her and not the other way round.

'No, Jean, I'm sure there isn't anything wrong,' she replied calmly, 'but a few unnatural-looking cells have shown up and I want to get them checked out. I shall be ringing the hospital this morning to arrange an appointment for you. . .'

'Unnatural?' Jean paused. 'Do you mean cancer?' she asked bluntly.

'At this stage, no,' replied Francesca firmly. 'But they could be indicating a pre-cancerous condition. I want you checked, Jean, so that if that is the case you get the right treatment.'

There was a silence on the other end of the phone.

'Jean?'

'Should I tell Jeff?'

'I don't see why not.' Francesca paused. 'There really isn't anything to worry about. Besides, he'll want to know. He'll want to go with you when you go for your appointment.'

'Yes, I suppose so.' Jean sounded doubtful, and, after saying goodbye, hung up.

With a sigh Francesca replaced the receiver then almost immediately lifted it again and asked the receptionist on duty to get the outpatient appointments department at the local hospital for her.

The rest of the day was frantically busy with full surgeries for them all and little sign of an easing of the tourist situation.

As Francesca and Guy wearily left the clinic at the end of the day he tossed his case on to the back seat of his car and said, 'I could murder a pint.'

'OK,' Francesca nodded, 'we'll nip into the pub on the way home.' She paused as Ros came out of the building and locked the front door behind her. 'Care to join us, Ros?' she called.

Ros looked up quickly. She too looked tired. 'Join you?' She looked faintly startled.

'Yes,' it was Guy who answered, winding his window

down and smiling at Ros, 'the Sportsman's Rest, for a quick drink.'

'Well, I don't know. . .' Ros hesitated.

'Oh, come on, I think we've all earned it today,' said Guy, leaning back and opening the rear door of the Rover.

'Oh, all right.' Ros suddenly looked pleased. 'I dare say Mum will be OK for another hour or so. My aunt is with her today.'

'Are you finding it hard to cope?' asked Francesca as she took her place next to Guy after locking her own car.

'Well, it isn't getting any easier, let's put it that way,' replied Ros with a grimace. 'I was up most of last night with her—she just didn't seem to realise it was night-time.'

'Ros's mother has Alzheimer's disease,' Francesca explained to Guy as he drove out of the car park.

'Most days now she hardly remembers who I am,' said Ros from the back seat.

'I can sympathise with that,' said Guy grimly, then when neither of them spoke he said, 'Would it be better if she was in care?'

'Yes, I'm sure it would.' Ros sighed.

'Would she be reluctant to go?' asked Guy.

'No.' Ros shrugged. 'It isn't that; in fact, I don't think she'd even realise. . .I suppose it's me, really. . .I just hate the thought of it; I've cared for her for a long time now and somehow it would seem like giving in. . .but quite apart from that, places are few and far between. . .and I would want her near by.'

A few minutes later they drove on to the forecourt of Bletchley Bridge's local pub, the Sportsman's Rest. A grey stone building with green and gold striped awnings over its windows, it had baskets of wallflowers hanging either side of the doorway and menu boards propped against the wall. It had been raining during the day; puddles dotted the car park and the wrought-iron chairs and tables in the pub's garden were deserted, their coloured umbrellas tightly furled.

The bar, in contrast, was packed with both tourists and locals. The appetising smell of hot cooked food wafted from the pub's kitchen and mingled with the smell of wet plastic raincoats. A group of hikers got up from a window table, and while Guy went to the bar to order drinks Francesca and Ros thankfully sat down.

As Guy was returning to the table, wending his way through the crowd, holding aloft a tray of drinks, a man suddenly detached himself from a group around the bar and made his way towards them.

'Well, hello there,' he said as Guy set the tray down. 'Now, if this isn't a coincidence!' The man was thickset, balding and around sixty years of age, and Francesca, who was watching Guy, knew instantly as he turned and looked at the man that he had no idea who he was. . .unfortunately neither did she.

'Hello.' Guy smiled, but it was an uncertain smile. 'How are you?'

Francesca flashed a look at Ros and saw that she also appeared to have read the situation. Questioningly she raised her eyebrows but Ros, very slightly, shook her head, the gesture indicating that she didn't know the man either.

'How am I?' the man was saying. 'Well, there's a question. That's why I said this was a coincidence, seeing you in here. I'd planned to come to see you tomorrow anyway. . .'

'Is that so?' said Guy politely. 'In that case I'll look forward to seeing you then.'

The man wasn't to be put off that easily, however. 'I said to the wife when it happened again, I said, Brenda, I'm going back to Bletchley. . . Dr Sinclair is the only one who's ever done me any good. She says I'm an old fool, that in the thousands of people you see you wouldn't remember me. But I told her not to be daft. I told her, how could he forget me? Like I said, Dr Sinclair, you're the only one who's ever done me any good. . .do you know that? Eh?' He looked from one to the other of them.

It was Ros who broke the desperate silence, a quick-thinking Ros. 'Do you know,' she said staring up at the man with interest, 'I've been sitting here trying to think where I'd seen you before...now I know; you came to the clinic, didn't you? Earlier this year... June, wasn't it?'

'No, May.' He looked pleased that Ros had apparently recognised him. 'We always visit the Lakes in May, me and Brenda.'

'Very sensible...it's a lovely time of the year. How far do you have to come... Mr... Mr...? I'm sorry, do you know, your name quite escapes me...?' Ros gave a light little laugh and shrugged.

'Well, you can't be expected to remember everyone's name, can you?' he said seriously. 'Not in a job like yours. The name's Billows, George Billows,' he puffed his cheeks out and gave an old-fashioned little bow as he said it, then he added, 'From Altrincham, miss.'

'Of course,' said Ros. 'How silly of me to forget. Well, Mr Billows, at least I shall know who you are when you come and see us tomorrow, won't I?'

As George Billows moved back to the bar Guy, with obvious relief, sat down and took a sip of his beer. 'Cheers, Ros,' he said, 'thanks for that. I didn't have a clue who he was.'

'I know,' Ros muttered, 'and to be honest I didn't remember him either.'

'That was clever of you, getting his name and where he comes from,' said Francesca, raising her own glass, taking a sip then setting it down on the table.

'Well, when he talked about Guy being the only doctor who had done him any good it sounded as if his complaint could be a bit unusual. I thought there might be a problem with that,' said Ros. 'But if we have his name and his home town I might be able to trace his GP, who should have a record of what Guy prescribed for him.'

'Good thinking,' said Francesca.

'I wonder why his own GP hasn't reissued the medication, whatever it was,' mused Guy before taking another sip of his beer.

'Well, don't worry about it,' said Ros. 'I'll start ringing round first thing in the morning. . .' She glanced at the door as she was speaking and trailed off.

Francesca looked over her shoulder to see who had caught Ros's attention and saw that David had just come into the pub. 'Oh, look who's arrived!' She laughed. 'At this rate all the clinic staff will soon be in here.' She half stood up and waved to attract his attention. 'Come and join us, David,' she called.

He was grinning as he fought his way through the crowd. 'So this is where you all get to,' he said, grabbing an empty chair from another table and drawing it forward.

'What are you having?' Guy stood up.

'Oh, a pint, I think,' replied David. 'Yes, it's been one of those days that should definitely end with a pint.'

Guy moved to the bar, and as David sat down Francesca glanced at Ros and was intrigued to see that her cheeks had grown quite pink.

When Guy returned the talk turned to a new conservation programme that had recently been set up in the area. It was an unwritten law among themselves that neither practice business nor patients should ever be discussed in public.

When eventually Francesca finished her drink and looked up she found Guy watching her. Instinctively she knew what he was thinking and as a look of mutual understanding passed between them Guy stood up and drained his glass.

'We really must be going,' he said, then, looking down at Ros, he added, 'Oh, I'm sorry, Ros, you haven't finished your drink—would you mind if we shoot off and leave you with David?'

'No, no, of course not.' Ros looked faintly startled.

'That's OK,' said David, 'I can run Ros home. . . but can't I get you two a drink first?' He looked from one to the other of them.

'No really,' Francesca stood up, 'we must be going. Guy's on call. See you both tomorrow.' She smiled at each of them in turn, then as Guy raised his hand in farewell she followed him out of the bar, almost stumbling in her haste.

George Billows waved enthusiastically to them as they passed, and as if he was suddenly afraid that the man was about to launch into another assault Guy grabbed her hand and they literally ran across the car park, sidestepping the puddles. He opened the car door for her and Francesca collapsed into the passenger-seat.

'I thought we went in there for a quiet drink,' she gasped, 'to get away from things. There's been more tension and drama in the last half-hour than we've had all week!'

Guy laughed. 'You're right—but I told you, didn't I, about Ros? Did you see the way she coloured up when David came in?'

'I did. . .along with your all too obvious attempt at matchmaking!'

'Well,' he grinned suddenly, 'David's impossible! He just doesn't see what's staring him in the face.'

When Francesca didn't answer he threw her a sidelong glance. 'You don't approve?' he asked. 'Of my matchmaking, as you call it?'

'It's not that I don't approve, it's that I still don't understand how you picked this thing up and the rest of us didn't.'

'Ah, it must be my highly developed sense of perception.' He grinned again. 'Anyway, we'll see what comes of tonight.'

'He's only going to run her home, for goodness' sake,' she protested. 'there's not a lot can come from that.'

'You don't think so?' He raised one eyebrow and threw her a cryptic glance. 'Ros was looking particularly radiant tonight, especially after David joined us, and you mark my words, when David realises how she feels about him everything will change—it's the greatest aphrodisiac of all, knowing someone thinks you're wonderful.'

'Is this the voice of experience talking?' She threw him an amused glance.

'Not particularly.' He laughed. 'It's just because we are happy and I want everyone else to be.'

Francesca smiled at him. 'Well, I suppose we'll just have to wait and see what happens.' She fell silent for a moment, then said thoughtfully, 'That was quick thinking on Ros's part with that man Billows, wasn't it?'

'Yes, it was,' he agreed. 'But...'

'What's the matter?' She threw him a quick look but he was leaning forward, concentrating on the road, looking from right to left as they drew out of the pub car park.

'I don't know.' He settled back into his seat. 'I just get the feeling it's not going to be straightforward where that man is concerned.'

'Oh, I'm sure it'll be all right.' She hoped she sounded reassuring. 'Once you know what medication you prescribed, it'll be fine. Maybe it was something his GP is unfamiliar with, a drug that isn't used very much in this country—something you used in America.'

'Yes,' he nodded, 'I wondered if it could be that. You're probably right, but...I still wish I could remember—it's so frustrating.'

'I know,' she said softly. 'But we're winning, Guy. I'm sure we're winning.' She placed her hand on his thigh and he took one hand from the steering-wheel to cover it, squeezing it tightly.

'Thanks to you,' he murmured, his voice suddenly husky.

Because Francesca had left her car at the clinic overnight, the following morning Guy dropped her off at the surgery before going on to make an early-morning house call.

She made her way to her consulting-room and as she passed Ros's office door the practice manager called out to her.

'There are several G. Billows in Altrincham,' she said, 'but I'm working through the list. Luckily our temporary residents' surgery today isn't until this afternoon, so by then hopefully I might have found something out.'

'Well done, Ros.' Francesca paused. 'Guy will be pleased; he really doesn't want to have to admit that he can't remember not only the medication, but the patient himself!'

'There won't be any need for that—we'll get the information somehow.'

'Thanks. . .' She was about to turn away, to continue to her own room and face the mountain of post that would inevitably be awaiting her, but something made her stop. 'Are you all right, Ros?' she asked, peering curiously at the other woman.

'Yes.' Ros answered quickly, too quickly. 'Why? Why do you ask?'

'I don't know.' Francesca hesitated. 'There's something different about you this morning. . . you seem. . .I don't know. . .extra happy or something. . .almost glowing, in fact. . .' She trailed off, aware that the smile on Ros's face had turned into a laugh, a bubbling, radiant laugh. 'There is something. . .!'

'What?' Ros raised her eyebrows in a questioning but secretive gesture. Then she gave a happy little shrug. 'Oh, what the hell? I might as well tell you. . . David has asked me out.'

'Really?' Francesca tried to look suitably surprised.

'Yes, last night. . .after you'd gone. We had a couple of drinks and, well, one thing led to another. He took me home, then he asked me to have dinner with him at the weekend.'

'So how do you feel about that?' Francesca feigned innocence then laughed and said, 'As if I need to ask—one look at your face is enough. . .'

'I've felt like it for years. . .' Ros admitted ruefully.

'Well, I must say you're a dark horse; I would never have guessed——' She was about to go on to say that

Guy had guessed, when Ros interrupted.

'I never thought I stood a chance with David, at least not with you around.' She gave a rueful smile.

'Me——?' Francesca began to protest, but Ros cut her short.

'Come on, Francesca, David used to think the sun shone out of you; he never spared a glance for anyone else. . . But then, when you fell head over heels for Guy. . .I thought, maybe at last David will notice I'm alive.'

'Oh, Ros!' Francesca stared at her. 'Whyever didn't you say. . .tell someone. . .?'

'I couldn't. You know me, I've always been so shy; I'm just not assertive like that lot in there.' Ros nodded towards Reception, where the sound of laughter could be heard from the other receptionists.

'And none of them guessed?' asked Francesca in amazement. 'Usually the faintest whisper sets them off.'

'No.' Ros shook her head, then softly she added, 'Only Guy knew.'

'Guy?' Francesca paused.

'Yes. I told him once in a mad moment, then regretted it. But he knew it was in confidence and I knew he wouldn't betray a confidence. . .anyway,' she seemed to visibly pull herself together, 'it's early days yet, nothing may come of it, this sort of thing has happened before. . .and let's face it, I still have my mother to think of. Quite honestly it's reaching the stage where I'm having to do almost everything for her. . .not just the cooking and cleaning—I've done that sort of thing for years—but washing and bathing her now as well. . .it's not easy for anyone to understand. . .'

'David's a doctor,' said Francesca quietly; 'he will understand.'

'Even so. . .' Ros left the sentence unfinished and turned as her phone began to ring.

Francesca made her way to her room. So Guy had been right about Ros's feelings for David, but it hadn't been as they had thought, simply observation or even intuition. Ros had said she had actually told him. And if that was the case—a sudden jolt of realisation shot through her—it meant that Guy must have remembered, if not Ros's actually telling him, then what she had told him.

This was the first positive memory he'd had of that shadowy period of time that had remained a closed book to him.

And he hadn't even recognised it as such.

Suddenly desperate to tell him, she looked out of the window to see if his car was in the car park, but there was no sign of the red Rover. Turning back to her desk, she stared down at her morning mail with unseeing eyes, her brain teeming.

Was it the first of many memories? Would others follow, and, if so, would they follow slowly, or would they crowd back in a frightening surge? Her knees felt suddenly weak and she sank down on to her chair.

She had no further opportunity to see Guy before surgery, as her own patients were arriving before he had returned from his house call. In the end it was nearly lunchtime before she made her way into Reception.

'Has my husband finished his surgery yet?' she asked Fiona, the youngest of the receptionists.

'Not quite, Dr Sinclair,' replied Fiona, glancing at the appointments book. 'He has his last patient with him now.'

'OK, Fiona, thanks—is Ros around?'

'Yes, she's in her office.' The girl nodded across the reception area towards the closed door of Ros's office.

Francesca crossed the floor, tapped on the door and pushed it open. Ros was standing by the fax machine, reading a report. She glanced up as Francesca came into the room. 'You'll be pleased to know we've got the necessary information on George Billows,' she said.

'Oh, well done, Ros,' Francesca replied, 'Guy will be relieved. Did you speak to his GP?'

'I did.' Ros nodded.

'So what did he say?' Francesca was curious. 'Why didn't he repeat what Guy had prescribed?'

'It wasn't quite as easy as that.' Ros frowned. 'Here, see for yourself—his surgery have just faxed this through.'

Francesca took the piece of paper that Ros handed her and quickly scanned it. 'I see what you mean,' she said after a moment, then without looking up she added, 'I think I'd better give this to Guy myself.'

'I was hoping you'd say that,' replied Ros with a grimace.

Slowly Francesca made her way to the door, still looking at the paper. 'Thank, Ros,' she said over her shoulder, 'and well done.'

Guy was still in his room, sitting at his desk, when she tapped on the door and stuck her head round.

'It's you,' he said, his expression softening as he caught sight of her. 'I was about to say "no more", but in your case I could make an exception... What can I do for you, Dr Sinclair?'

'I think it's more a case of what I can do for you...'

'Oh, I don't doubt that.' He grinned, and Francesca flushed.

'Will you behave yourself just for one moment, please?' she said with mock-severity.

'Sure.' He nodded and leaned back in his chair. 'Only for one moment, mind. Then can I do what I like?' He gave a wicked chuckle, paused, then looked at the paper she was holding in her hand. 'What have you got there?'

'A copy of the treatment you prescribed for George Billows.'

'Really?' He sat up straight.

'Yes,' Francesca replied coolly. 'I thought that might make you pay attention. Ros got it for you.'

'May I see?' He stretched out his hand and Francesca found herself hesitating. 'Well, come on, then.' A half-smile curved his lips. 'What's wrong? Did I give the poor fellow some obscure hill-billy remedy that no one's ever heard of in this country?'

Francesca shook her head. 'No, it's a little more than that,' she said, handing him the paper.

'What do you mean?' Guy was looking at her as he took the paper, his expression wary as if he sensed her apprehension.

'See for yourself,' She nodded at the paper, and when he looked down she added, 'It's not exactly medication—rather, hands-on treatment.'

Guy was silent as he studied the report.

'I didn't know you did manipulation,' said Francesca at last when he still didn't speak.

'Neither did I,' he replied bluntly. At last he looked up and met her gaze.

'Oh, dear.' Francesca leaned forward and took the paper from his grasp again. 'I was afraid you might be going to say that. But. . .that's definitely what it says here.' Looking down, she read from the paper. '"Manipulation of the spine for bulging disc."'

Guy continued to stare at her for a long moment, his face expressionless, then got up and walked to the window, where he stood looking out at the neat flower borders round the clinic's car-park.

'What would you normally prescribe for that?' asked Francesca.

'I belong to the "rest and pain-killer brigade",' replied Guy slowly, then, turning from the window, he said, 'at least, I thought I did. Now, who knows?' He gave a helpless, almost angry shrug. 'I'm not sure of anything any more.' When she remained silent he went on, 'Honestly, Francesca, I had no idea so much could happen in the space of eighteen months—so many things to change not only one's life, but also, it seems, the habits of a lifetime.'

'Maybe,' she said hopefully, 'it was just a spot of massage you did at George Billows' request.'

Guy shook his head and turned back to the window, the gesture full of frustration. 'It sounds more than that,' he said tightly.

'Well, at least you know what the condition is before the patient comes back. Just think what it would have been like if you hadn't...you really would have been at a disadvantage then. As it is, now you will know what line of questioning to take,' she added.

'I suppose so.' He turned to face her again and she was filled with sudden despair as she saw that the bleak look was back in his eyes. The look that had all but disappeared recently. 'Not that I know how I shall handle it if he wants more manipulation...I really can't recall ever giving manipulation before...still, it was good of Ros to find out for me,' he added flatly.

Francesca looked up sharply at the mention of Ros's name and in sudden desperation—anything to bring the hope back into his eyes—she said, 'Talking of Ros, you were quite right there, you know.'

'What?' He frowned vaguely as if his mind was still on George Billows.

'About her and David,' Francesca persisted. 'She is in love with him, and guess what! He's asked her out!'

'Well, thank goodness I still have my powers of observation or intuition or whatever it was,' he said bitterly.

'No, Guy.' She couldn't hide her excitement any longer. 'You don't understand: there's more to it than that.'

'What do you mean?' His eyes narrowed.

She took a deep breath, 'Ros said she told you the way she felt about David.'

'Told me?' He was still frowning.

'Apparently so.'

'But why? Why me?'

'I don't know. Maybe she wanted a shoulder to cry on and you happened to be there at the time...I don't know...she said she told you in confidence, which implies she hadn't told anyone else...but that's not it, Guy. The point I'm getting at,' she struggled to keep calm, 'is *when* she told you, not why.' He stared at her blankly. 'Don't you see?' she went on excitedly. 'It must have been at some time before we were married. And for you to have known, for you to have been aware of Ros's feelings for David means you must have remembered, if not her actually telling you, then what she told you.'

He was silent for a long moment.

'Guy. . .?' she said at last.

'It still could have just been intuition,' he said slowly, dubiously.

'I don't think so.' She rushed on, even more excited now as the realisations took deeper root. 'If it had been that obvious, surely one of us would have noticed? After all, we all know Ros and David so well. As it was, none of us suspected a thing. . .whereas you. . .you, who had only recently arrived on the scene. . .you knew.'

'I didn't know at the beginning,' he said slowly, sitting down abruptly in his chair again and staring up at Francesca. 'Not when we first came back from Spain; I don't think I was aware of it then.'

'Maybe not,' she replied patiently. 'But you were aware of some emotion towards David—you were even surprised you'd asked him to be your best man.'

'I told you I thought that was because I'd realised he'd fancied you at one time.'

'I don't think it was that. You were fine with David over that when he first came back from his sabbatical—you even joked about it. No, Guy, it wasn't that; don't forget, you were lodging at David's, so you were in his company quite a lot. I think you had developed a sense of irritation towards him for being so obtuse over Ros after what she had told you.'

'But I wasn't aware of what Ros had told me. . .'

'Not at that point no. But don't you see. . .somewhere along the line you did remember. . .the emotion first, then the knowledge? A part of your memory returned! You weren't aware of when it happened—it just did. And that, I'm sure, is what will happen. It's what Helen Ryder said. . .it'll come back gradually, almost without your being aware of it.'

He continued to stare at her, then, 'Oh God,' he muttered, 'it's terrifying.'

'But exciting.' Leaning across the desk, Francesca

took his hands. 'It's starting to happen, Guy,' she whispered urgently, 'what we hoped for. Your memory is starting to return!'

CHAPTER ELEVEN

FRANCESCA was out on a house call when George Billows came to see Guy, and when she returned the door to her husband's room was firmly closed. Almost immediately she was caught up in the demands of her weekly baby clinic, and although she was dying to ask Guy how he had got on she knew she would just have to wait until later.

In the end it was Guy who came to see her. She had just given the last baby its triple vaccine and was washing her hands.

'Oh, there you are,' she said, her heart sinking as she noticed how drawn he looked. 'I was just coming to find you—how did you get on with George. . .?'

He shook his head and she indicated for him to come right into the room and shut the door. It wouldn't do for this particular conversation to be overheard and possibly misconstrued.

'I didn't know what the hell he was talking about,' he said bluntly as he turned from the door.

'Oh, Guy. That bad.' She stared at him in dismay. 'I was hoping you might have been able to bluff your way through.' He shrugged, the gesture giving nothing away. 'But he's gone now. . .?' Francesca glanced apprehensively at the door almost as if she half expected George Billows to suddenly materialise.

'Oh, yes, he's gone,' said Guy, 'but he'll be back.'

'Back? You mean. . .?'

'Oh, yes, apparently when I saw him before I gave him two sessions of manipulation a few days apart, and I appear to have worked some sort of miracle where everyone else had failed.' He pulled a face and sat down heavily on the chair opposite her desk. Folding his arms, he stared moodily into space.

In silence Francesca finished drying her hands,

disposing of the paper towel in the waste-bin before turning to face him. 'So did you attempt this manipulation, or whatever it was?' she asked, curious as to how he had coped.

'What?' He looked up at her as if he hadn't heard what she'd said, as if his mind had been far away in some strange twilight zone of its own.

'The manipulation?' she repeated patiently. 'Did you have a go?' Her heart sank even further as she realised Guy's mood seemed to be reverting to the almost depressive condition it had reached following the accident—the condition that had improved so much recently.

He stared at her. 'Oh, yes,' he replied absent-mindedly at last as the meaning of her question seemed to sink in, 'I had a go.'

'And?' She waited, and when he didn't elaborate she said, 'How did it go?'

'Oh, I do a brilliant line in miracles—didn't you know?' There was no disguising the sarcasm in his voice and Francesca flinched.

'I was only asking——'

'Well, honestly, Francesca, how do you think it went?' He stared at her in exasperation. 'I get a patient I don't know from Adam who tells me I'm the only doctor who has ever put him right. He lies on my couch, puts his total trust in me and expects me to carry out a procedure I don't recall ever doing in my life before!'

'I'm sorry, Guy,' she said quietly. 'I was concerned, that's all.'

'Yes, and I'm concerned,' he said angrily, standing up. 'Bloody concerned. I don't know how I ever thought I could get away with this charade... how I ever let the rest of you talk me into believing I could.'

'But you were doing fine until this,' cried Francesca, holding on to the back of her desk for support. 'You mustn't let this one incident put you back——'

'One incident? Did you say one incident?' He had

turned away from her towards the door but he swung round now.

'Well, that's all it is...' she began uncertainly, almost frightened by the bitter anger in his eyes.

'Is it? Just one incident. So that's all you think it is? Eh?' he demanded. 'So what about the lapse of confidentiality I'm guilty of?' He'd lowered his voice now. 'Doesn't that count?'

'What do you mean?' She frowned at him in bewilderment.

'That is something I've never been guilty of in all my professional career...until now.'

'Guy,' she took a deep breath as it suddenly dawned on her what he meant, 'if you're talking about Ros——?'

'Of course I'm talking about Ros.' He cut her short then and, the frown lines deepening between his eyes, he said suspiciously, 'Why? Have there been other incidents, other betrayals that I'm unaware of?'

'No, of course not——'

'How do you know? How do I know? How does anyone know if I myself can't remember what I was told?'

In the silence that followed there came the sounds of laughter from a group of children outside the clinic, and when Francesca didn't reply Guy went on in a kind of brutal desperation as if he knew in some way that ultimately there could be no compromise for his condition, 'And if by some obscure chance,' his voice was still low, 'I do find myself remembering the facts, but not whether or not I was told those facts in confidence...what then?' Still Francesca didn't reply. 'God only knows what Ros thinks of me for betraying her as it is.' He turned away again.

'Ros doesn't think that.' At last Francesca spoke.

'What?' he turned again and stared at her.

'She doesn't think you told me,' she said quietly.

'So how does she think you found out?' he demanded.

'She doesn't think I found out at all,' she said

patiently, then added, 'In fact, she told me herself.'

He continued to stare at her almost as if he didn't believe her, then shrugged. 'It doesn't really make a lot of difference, does it? What she thinks happened and what actually did happen. I did betray her confidence and that's that.'

'But it was unknowingly,' Francesca protested, her heart going out to him in his frustration.

'Since when was ignorance any sort of defence?'

'But it's not even as if Ros is your patient.'

'That's neither here nor there,' he said harshly. 'She could well have been. It would have made no difference to the facts. I still wouldn't have known, just as I still can't know if there have been others I've betrayed, or may betray, in the future.'

'You're being too hard on yourself, Guy,' Francesca protested. 'Unnecessarily hard.'

'I don't think so.' An obstinate note had crept into his voice.

'So what are you saying?' Leaning her clenched fists on the polished woodwork, Francesca faced him across the desk.

'What am I saying?' He shrugged. 'I don't know. Probably that I shouldn't be practising.'

'Don't say that, Guy.' She was aware of the pleading note that had crept into her voice. 'Not after all your efforts. . .after everyone's efforts.'

He remained silent for a long moment, apparently struggling with his thoughts, then gave a shrug. 'Maybe what I mean,' he said, 'is that I shouldn't practise until more of my memory returns.'

'And if it doesn't?' she asked softly.

'I don't know!' His voice rose suddenly and her eyes flickered warningly towards the door, but, oblivious to the possibility of being overheard, oblivious to everything, he shouted, 'I don't know! For God's sake, Francesca, I just don't know!' Turning sharply, he angrily wrenched open the door and strode from the room, almost colliding with a startled Fiona, who was standing outside, her hand raised to knock on the door.

The girl was left staring at Francesca, who faced her across the desk.

'I'm sorry,' Francesca muttered helplessly. 'Sorry, Fiona, you'll have to excuse him, he's a bit overwrought today.' Then with a superhuman effort she attempted to pull herself together. 'You were looking for me?'

'Yes.' With an apprehensive glance over her shoulder, Fiona nodded and said, 'Maureen Fellows has been on the phone from Peacehaven. Apparently Em—Mrs Addison—is very poorly; having problems with her breathing.'

'I'll call in on my way home,' said Francesca. 'Oh, and Fiona, shut the door on your way out, please.'

'Of course.'

As the girl went back to Reception Francesca sank wearily down on to her chair.

Guy was silent and withdrawn for the rest of that day, even during their meal that evening, in spite of Francesca's attempts to maintain a light-hearted conversation.

And later, when she asked if he was coming to bed, he replied abruptly without looking at her, 'Not yet. You go on up.'

She lay awake for a long time, only too aware of the renewed turmoil he was going through, but at the same time knowing she was powerless to help him. In the end, exhausted by the day's events and before Guy came to bed, she fell asleep.

She was awakened by the ringing of the telephone. Daylight was filtering through the curtains, the hands of the clock stood at six and the space beside her, though rumpled, was empty. Sleepily she lifted the receiver.

'Hello?' she mumbled. 'Dr Sinclair speaking.'

The caller was a young schoolteacher from Ambleside who feared his wife was having a miscarriage.

'Tell her to stay in bed,' said Francesca after he'd given her the details. 'I'll be over to see her as soon as I can.' Getting out of bed, she stumbled to the bathroom.

When she got downstairs there was no sign of Guy; then she remembered it was his day off and that he had probably gone for an early-morning walk. The percolator was still hot, so she poured herself a mug of coffee then dialled the Peacehaven number on the kitchen telephone. An unfamiliar voice answered.

'Good morning,' Francesca said, 'Dr Sinclair here. Could I speak to Mrs Fellows, please?'

'I'm sorry,' the voice replied, 'Mrs Fellows is not on duty yet.'

'I see.' She paused. 'Well, maybe you can tell me how Mrs Addison is this morning.'

'I'm afraid I don't really know——' the voice sounded doubtful '——I'm just doing the early-morning tea; could you ring back when Mrs Fellows is here?'

'When will that be?' Francesca suppressed a sigh. Em had really been quite poorly the previous evening when she had called in to see her and she'd arranged for her to have some oxygen to assist with her breathing.

'She comes on duty at seven...but if you'd like to hang on, I'll see if her deputy is around.'

'No, it's all right,' replied Francesca briskly. 'I'll ring back around seven.'

There had been a ground frost during the night and the heavy dew clung to the blades of grass on the front lawn, sparkling on dozens of spider's webs that festooned the rose bushes. The sun was struggling through the soft early-morning mist but as Francesca drove away from the cottage her heart was heavy, for there was still no sign of Guy and she knew she wouldn't now see him until evening.

The beauty of Lake Windermere in the soft light of the autumn morning was almost lost on Francesca, so immersed was she in her own troubles, but when she reached the house on the outskirts of Ambleside and found her patient, Julie Ryan, bleeding heavily her own worries were immediately forgotten as her professionalism took over.

'We need to get her into hospital,' she said to the girl's frantic husband after examining her. 'If I can use your phone I'll ring for an ambulance.'

Francesca waited until the ambulance arrived and her patient was comfortable and on her way to hospital, then she got back into the car and began to drive back to Bletchley Bridge. It had been her intention to drive straight to the clinic and to ring Maureen Fellows from there, but when she glanced at her watch it was to find that it was only twenty past seven. On a sudden impulse as she approached the bridge she decided to go back to the cottage and see if Guy had returned.

As she entered the cottage she heard the sound of running water and realised that it was the shower. She decided to wait. To fill in the time, she could make her call to Peacehaven.

Perching on one of the tall kitchen stools, she lifted the receiver and pressed the redial button, fully expecting to hear Maureen Fellows' voice as the phone was answered. Instead, there was a series of clicks on the line, then faintly, but clearly, Francesca heard an unfamiliar female voice.

'This is Chloe Steinburg. Sorry I'm not available to take your call. If you leave your name and number I'll call you back just as soon as I can.'

The voice had a nasal twang, but an unmistakable American accent. Francesca stared at the phone in bewilderment, then as realisation dawned she dropped the receiver as if it had burnt her fingers. With her heart hammering and still staring at the phone, she got up from the stool.

Chloe?

Chloe Steinburg? Was that her name?

Probably. Francesca didn't know. But that was immaterial. What was more to the point was why had she been rung when Francesca had pressed the redial button? The last number she had called had been Peacehaven's.

As the only possible explanation dawned on her she looked up the stairs. From the sounds that were still coming from the bathroom she knew Guy to be still in the shower.

She closed her eyes. Her hands curled involuntarily into tight fists at her sides.

Why had he tried to call Chloe?

Suddenly sick at heart, she turned away. She needed time to think.

No, she must ask him now. Must know the truth. There was most likely some simple explanation. She stood at the foot of the stairs, one hand on the newel post, looking up. The bathroom door was tightly closed.

If there was a simple explanation, why hadn't he told her he was going to phone? Why had he waited until she was out of the house before making his call?

A thin line of sweat broke out on her upper lip. She must ask him about this if only to put her mind at rest. There had to be some simple explanation.

But, some little demon goaded, what if this wasn't the first time he'd called the American woman. . .what if he'd been calling her all along?

Somewhere, unbidden, in the back of her mind she heard a voice, Marie's voice saying, 'I think he's having us all on. I don't think he's lost his memory at all.' Her heart was thumping now, the blood pounding in her head. They'd laughed about it at the time. Marie had called it spooky. But suppose it was true? Suppose he really hadn't lost his memory, only pretended he had? What if he was pretending he didn't remember her, when all along he did?

No! Her hand flew to her mouth. It couldn't be. The idea was too ludicrous, too far-fetched. It was impossible. Guy would never do that. Besides, what possible motive could he have for doing such a thing? What could he possibly gain from it? Nothing. Absolutely nothing.

So why had he secretly phoned the American woman? Why was he still in contact with her?

Suddenly she heard the click of the shower screen and knew that Guy had finished, would soon be opening the bathroom door, would look down the stairs and see her standing at the bottom.

Almost choking on the acid-tasting bile that had suddenly risen in her throat, she turned and fled, out of the cottage, down the path and into her car. With hands that trembled and not even waiting to fasten her seatbelt, she switched on the engine, shot it into gear and roared away.

She'd calmed down a little by the time she reached the surgery as her natural common sense took over. She was the first to arrive, which wasn't surprising, given the earliness of the hour, and after she had finally got through to Maureen Fellows and checked that there was no deterioration in Em's condition she made herself a badly needed coffee and retreated to her consulting-room to think.

Firmly she told herself that it was sheer lunacy to even suspect that Guy might not have lost his memory—the notion was quite simply unthinkable. There could not have been any possible motive for him to do so, she told herself firmly.

But, once that idea was firmly relegated to where it belonged, she still needed to know why he would have put through a call to Chloe. Did he think she could be the key to his regaining his memory? When he had got the message on her answerphone, had he left their own number so she could call him back? Was he even now talking to this woman, the woman he had admitted to dating while he had been in the States, the woman whose name he'd said just after the accident, when Helen Ryder had told him his wife had come to see him?

If she closed her eyes Francesca could still see him sitting in that cane chair by the window in that hospital room in Spain. Could still see the expression on his face, one almost of incredulity as he had looked at Helen Ryder before he'd caught sight of her, Francesca, then that same expression changing to one of blankness when he'd turned his head and failed to recognise her.

Oh, God! She shuddered; she mustn't think about that again.

Guy loved her, she knew that. He'd loved her when he'd first come here, loved her enough to marry her, and he loved her again now. . .she was sure he did. . .

But just supposing he'd loved Chloe as well. . . supposing——?

She jumped as someone suddenly knocked on her door, startling her out of her jumbled thoughts.

'Come in,' she called abruptly, looking up as the door opened.

David stood on the threshold. 'Hello,' he said, 'you're early this morning. . .' He frowned as he saw her expression. 'Is everything all right?'

'Yes,' she said quickly, then, seeing his raised eyebrows, she said again, 'yes, fine, David.'

He stood in the doorway, watching her, making no attempt either to go or to come into the room and give a reason for his visit.

'Did you want something?' she asked at last.

'No, not really. I just wondered if you were all right, that's all.'

'Yes, like I said. . .I'm fine. . .' To her dismay her voice wavered.

'But it's not all plain sailing, is it?' David said quietly.

'No.' She managed a rueful smile. 'No, it isn't,' she admitted.

David came right into the room, shut the door behind him and perched on the edge of the desk. 'Come on,' he said gently, 'tell me about it.'

'I don't want to burden you with it all. . .'

'I don't mind, really I don't. Besides, isn't that what friends are for?'

'I suppose so.' She sighed then shot him a grateful glance. There was something so solid and dependable about David. 'It's just,' she said at last, 'that when I think we have things sorted out, something else comes along and rocks the boat.'

'Has he remembered anything else?'

'Fragments...that's all, just fragments here and there that don't really add up to much.'

'That's probably worse for him than not being able to remember anything at all,' mused David thoughtfully.

'Yes,' she sighed again. 'I dare say it is.'

'Is there anything I can do to help?' he asked after a moment.

'No, I don't think so.' Francesca hesitated, his sympathetic concern almost her undoing, and suddenly she longed to tell him what had happened that morning, to confide in him, to seek his opinion, but somehow she resisted, feeling it would be disloyal to Guy. Instead, almost in an effort to hide her embarrassment, she found herself saying, 'I understand you and Ros are going out together.' David smiled and nodded. 'Well, I'm pleased. I hope it works out for you both.'

'It's strange how something can be right under your nose and you miss it, isn't it?' He glanced at his watch then stood up. 'I suppose I'd better be getting on,' he said and turned towards the door.

'David, wait. There is something...' On a sudden impulse she called him back.

'Yes?' He turned and looked at her.

'David, you've known Guy a long time,' she said slowly, and when he nodded in agreement she rushed on, not giving herself a chance to change her mind. 'Would you say he was capable of doing anything...' the words tumbled out '...anything underhand?'

'Guy? Underhand?' She was aware of David's apparent surprise as he stared at her, and although she nodded, miserably, she wished she hadn't asked.

'Well,' he said slowly, 'I suppose anyone is capable...but Guy?' He shrugged. 'To me, Guy has always been the epitome of the perfect English gentleman; you know, slightly aloof, a bit of a lad, but underneath as straight as a die.' He paused and ran a hand over his crisp dark hair. 'In fact, I think I'd go so far as to say...I would trust him with my life.'

'Thanks,' she replied simply, looking him in the eye, 'that's what I thought.'

'So,' he gave her a quizzical look, 'whatever it is you are worrying about—I would say you could almost certainly stop. OK?'

'OK.' Francesca nodded and managed a smile.

Somehow she got through the rest of the day; the endless list of patients, the house calls and finally an antenatal clinic. She had just bade farewell to the last expectant mother, when Ros phoned through to say that Jean Blake was being admitted to hospital the following day for a cone biopsy of the cervix.

'Good,' Francesca replied. 'At least they haven't wasted any time. Thank heavens Jean always came for regular smear tests. Thanks, Ros.' She flicked her intercom switch and glanced at her watch. It was time she was heading for home.

Home. And home meant Guy.

What would he say to her? Would he tell her he'd phoned Chloe in America? Had Chloe phoned him back? And, if so, would he tell her what had been said?

With a sigh she stood up and was just transferring some papers from her desk to her case when her phone rang.

'Dr Sinclair?'

'Yes, Fiona?'

'I have the matron from Peacehaven on the phone. She wants to speak to you.'

'Very well, Fiona. Put her through.' She waited, heard a click then Maureen Fellows' voice.

'Maureen?'

'Dr Sinclair. It's Em, I'm afraid. She's deteriorating.'

'I'll be over in a few minutes.'

'Thank you. Oh, and Doctor, there was just one other thing...' Maureen hesitated and Francesca noticed the note of uncertainty in her voice.

'What is it, Maureen?'

'Well, earlier on Em was asking for your husband.'

'My husband?' She was aware of the surprise in her voice.

'Yes. As you know, he visited here several times when he first came to Bletchley and Em took a real shine to him. She doesn't have any family of her own, and, well, we always do our best to carry out any last wishes.'

'Of course.' Francesca swallowed. 'I'll see what I can do.'

'But he isn't on duty today, is he?'

'You just leave it with me.'

She redialled and Guy answered immediately—almost as if he had been waiting for a call.

She mustn't think of that now.

'Guy?'

'Hello.' His voice softened on the second syllable. 'Are you on your way home?'

'Not exactly.'

'Oh.'

She thought she detected disappointment in his tone but couldn't be certain. 'It's Em, Guy,' she said.

'What's wrong?'

'Bronchial pneumonia has set in; she's sinking fast. I'm on my way there.'

'Poor Duchess,' he said softly. 'So you'll be late.'

'Yes. But Guy, there's something I thought you'd want to know.'

'Oh, what's that?'

'Apparently she's been asking for you.'

'I'll meet you there.' His reply was instantaneous.

When she drove through the gates of Peacehaven Francesca saw Percy skulking among the shiny leaves of the rhododendrons that lined the drive. When he caught sight of her he put his head down, pretending not to see her, almost as if by not acknowledging her presence, or the reason for it, he could ignore what was happening to Em.

Guy drove in seconds after her and as he climbed out of the Rover Francesca immediately noticed that he looked more relaxed than he had the previous day. A sudden wave of panic swept over her. She hardly dared to speculate what might have happened to make him appear that way. That would come later. For the present, Em was top priority.

Both Maureen Fellows and the community nurse were with Em, whose breathing, thanks to the oxygen, sounded less laboured than when Francesca had previously seen her. In fact the old lady looked calm and very peaceful as she lay high on her pillows, her face devoid of make-up now, her jewellery in its velvet box on her dressing-table.

'Hello, Em.' Francesca bent over her and the old lady's eyelids flickered. 'I've brought someone to see you.'

Guy moved forward and took one fragile, blue-veined hand from where it lay on the bedspread and held it between both of his. 'Hi, Duchess,' he said softly and for one moment recognition flared in the faded blue eyes.

He sat beside her, stroking her hand while Francesca gave her an injection to relieve pain from congestion.

'Has Percy been in to see her?' Francesca murmured to Maureen a little later as she replaced the drug packet in her case.

Maureen shook her head. 'No, he sends flowers in every morning, but he won't come in himself.'

It was almost dark and there was so sign of Percy when Francesca and Guy left Peacehaven half an hour later in their separate cars and drove home to the cottage.

Wearily Francesca dumped her case on the kitchen floor while Guy crossed to the cupboard and took out two glasses. Then, bending down to the fridge, he took out a bottle of sparkling wine.

'Ah,' he said, 'that's nicely chilled. I'm sure you won't say no to a glass?'

'I think I would prefer to shower and change first——' she began but he interrupted.

'No, please, Francesca, I need to talk to you now,' he said. 'This won't wait.' There was a note of suppressed excitement in his voice.

'This has a celebratory air about it.' Francesca's gaze flickered warily to the phone.

'I suppose you could say that.' Guy smiled as he poured the wine.

'Well, whatever the reason. . .' she hesitated '. . .you certainly seem happier than you did last night.'

'Ah,' he said, handing her one of the glasses. Then, lifting his own, he examined the contents. 'Last night. Yes, I'm sorry about last night, Francesca; I guess I was pretty unbearable again.'

She gave a slight shrug. 'I suppose you had cause to be uptight.'

'Maybe. . .but I shouldn't have taken it out on you. . .none of this is your fault. But,' he paused and shot her an apologetic glance, 'you see, what with the George Billows affair, and then the fact that I had spilled the beans on Ros, I got myself into a bit of a state.'

'Yes, you did,' she said softly, staring at him over the rim of her glass. 'Unnecessarily so.'

'Maybe. . .maybe not, but it was enough to make me realise I had to do something about it.'

'What do you mean?' Carefully she set her glass down on the worktop, wondering what she was about to hear.

'Well, I decided I needed to fill in a few more of the gaps.' He stopped as if he was waiting for her to ask him what he meant.

'Gaps?'

'Yes, great holes in my memory.' He nodded. 'Everyone here has helped by telling me what happened while I was in this country, but there were other blanks—a great chunk of time of which I had no recollection at all. A time when I was living and working in a totally different environment.'

She remained silent, wanting him to continue yet dreading what he might be about to tell her.

'I came to the conclusion,' he went on, oblivious to the turmoil her own thoughts were in, 'that if I was to try to fill in this time it might help, not necessarily with restoring my memory. . .but at least I would know what had happened to me.'

The blood had started to pound in her head again. 'So what did you do?' she asked at last. Even to herself her voice sounded small.

'I phoned the States,' he replied.

'You phoned the States.' She picked up her glass again simply for something to do.

'Yes. I should have done it before, I know that now. . .but you see, I was afraid to.'

'Why?' Her grip tightened on the stem of the wine glass.

'I was afraid what I was going to hear and I suppose I didn't want to admit to them what had happened to me.'

'And now?' She suddenly felt very hot.

'Now?' He laughed. 'All I can say now is that I wish I had done it before.' As he spoke he raised his glass.

'So. . .so who did you speak to?' she asked.

'Sorry?' He was sipping his wine, but he looked up and, seeing her expression, he stopped and lowered the glass. 'What do you mean?'

'When you phoned the States. Who did you speak to?'

'Oh. I phoned the hospital where I had been working. I spoke to a colleague, Sam Reynolds, and he put me straight on so many things. Honestly, Francesca, it was incredible. You have no idea.'

'Sam Reynolds? Just him?'

'What do you mean?' He was frowning at her now.

'Was he the only one you spoke to?'

'The only one? Yes, yes, of course,' he replied. A puzzled look crossed his face.

Sick at heart, she turned away.

CHAPTER TWELVE

'WHAT'S wrong? Francesca?'

'Nothing,' she heard herself say.

'So don't you want to know what he told me?'

Guy sounded so eager and he couldn't know she knew he was lying.

Not waiting for her to answer, he said, 'I was lucky to catch him; he was just going off duty. . .but he told me so much. . .' Smiling now, he set his glass down. 'You're not drinking your wine. Oh, poor love,' he said, suddenly looking concerned, 'you've only just got home and there's me rabbiting on. . . Let's go and sit down. You must be tired.'

'Not particularly. . .'

'Even so.' He took her glass, set it down beside his own then gently but firmly propelled her into the sitting-room, where she allowed herself to be guided on to the sofa. As if in a dream she waited while he went back to the kitchen, returning almost immediately with the wine glasses.

'Sam is a fantastic character——' he began.

'Had you remembered that?' she said curtly. 'Or is it something you've deduced simply by talking to him on the phone?' Her voice sounded bleak even to herself and for one moment Guy looked a little taken aback.

'I'd remembered Sam certainly,' he said slowly at last, 'because I met him when I first went to the States, but talking to him has helped, I think.'

'You mean you've remembered more?' She raised her eyebrows.

He shook his head. 'No, I haven't remembered more, but then I didn't expect to. That wasn't the reason I rang.'

'So what was the reason, Guy?' she said quietly.

'Like I said just now, I reached a point of. . .I don't

know...desperation, if you like...I felt I had to do something.'

'So what did he tell you, this Sam?' Francesca paused, waiting for his answer. When it didn't come she said, 'Did you own up to your amnesia?'

'Yes, I did,' he replied quietly.

She threw him a sharp glance. He was standing in front of the fireplace, his wine glass cradled in his hand as if it were a brandy glass. The only sound in the room was the ticking of the grandmother clock in the corner.

'I wasn't going to at first,' he continued at last. 'I imagined I could get what I needed to know simply through conversation, but I soon realised it was going to be hard going, so I made a snap decision and decided to come clean. It was so much easier after that.'

'What did he say? About your amnesia?' Suddenly Francesca was simply curious, forgetting for the moment that Guy might be hiding things from her or that she might be about to hear something she'd rather not.

'He was sympathetic...and very interested,' Guy went on. 'He's dealt with a similar case himself apparently.'

'And did that patient regain his memory?'

'It was a her, actually,' he took a sip of his drink, 'and no, she didn't,' he added quietly.

Francesca took a deep breath. 'What else did he tell you?'

'I told him about George Billows and he was able to explain the manipulation technique which he thought I would have used. It seems it's a technique that was developed by an osteopath at the hospital and has been used there pretty extensively ever since. Apparently I was so impressed with its success rate that I learned how to do it.'

'So do you feel confident to carry it out now?' She knew she sounded sceptical, but couldn't help it.

He gave a slight shrug. 'Well, perhaps not exactly confident, but certainly better than I did before. Sam is going to fax through some literature on the subject for me tomorrow, so I should be able to gen up a bit before poor old George comes back for his second lot of treatment.'

'So what else did he tell you?' Francesca asked and when he didn't immediately reply she threw him a glance, half fearful, only to find he was smiling broadly.

'He told me something quite extraordinary,' he replied, rocking back and forth on his heels.

Francesca swallowed. 'Really?' Her voice came out high pitched, squeaky. She cleared her throat. 'Really?' she said again.

'Yes.' Guy sounded excited now. 'He told me I could ski.'

'Ski?' She stared at him. She wasn't quite sure what she had expected him to say, but it certainly wasn't that.

'Yes,' he nodded, laughing, 'apparently I learnt while I was in the States.' He fell silent for a moment, staring into his glass, then he threw Francesca a quick look. 'Had I said anything about being able to ski? Before the accident, I mean?'

'I don't know...' she frowned, wrinkling her forehead, trying to remember '...I'm really not sure... you might have done...' She spread her hands helplessly. 'Now it's my memory playing up.'

'Ah, well, never mind,' Guy replied. 'But it will be interesting to see whether or not I can still do it—you know, a skill I actually learnt during the period of time I've lost. Funny thing is, skiing was always one of those things I wanted to do but had never quite got round to. Sam told me about a holiday a crowd of us went on—a winter sports holiday at some ski resort.'

Francesca found herself wondering if Chloe had been on that holiday. 'And you can't recall any of it?' She tried to keep the note of suspicion out of her voice but wasn't sure she had succeeded.

'No.' He shrugged again almost absent-mindedly, not seeming to notice her attitude, but at the same time she was quick to note that the air of depression that had returned during the last day or so seemed to have lifted. He was silent for a while as if battling with his thoughts, then, 'Sam told me something else,' he said softly at last.

This was it. Francesca took a gulp of her drink and put her glass down.

'He told me,' Guy went on, 'about Chloe.' He threw her a glance, but when she didn't reply he carried on, quickly, but apparently choosing his words with care. 'I told you that I remembered I'd been dating Chloe when I first went to the States?'

'Yes.'

'And that I couldn't remember anything else. . .?'

'Guy. . .I——'

'Well,' he swept on, giving her no chance to intervene, 'I must admit it has bothered me what I said when Helen Ryder told me my wife was there to see me. You have to appreciate the fact, Francesca, that in my mind I was right back there in the States in that period of time when I was dating Chloe. She had been keen to take the relationship further. . .'

'You never told me that. . .'

'I know.' He hesitated then went on, 'I suppose just for a moment there I feared I might have done just that. But, when I had time to think about it and after I'd learned what had happened to me since, I knew deep in my heart there was no way I would ever have asked Chloe to marry me. Anyway. . . Sam told me that Chloe finally got her doctor.'

Francesca stared up at him and to her amazement saw he was smiling. 'I don't understand. . .'

'Neither did I at first,' he replied drily, 'but Sam soon filled me in. Apparently Chloe had made up her mind years ago she was going to marry a doctor.'

'Any particular doctor?' she asked faintly.

'No, I don't think so.' A cryptic little smile still played around the corners of his mouth. 'Preferably, I believe,' he went on after a moment, 'one who was on his way to becoming a consultant.' He paused. 'It seems Chloe pounced on any newcomer who might eventually fit the bill. When I first arrived in the States I was totally unaware of this. In my innocence I began dating her. She wasn't, by the way, actually quite as mercenary as I'm making her sound. She was in all fairness very attractive; in fact. . .quite a girl, our Chloe.' He gave a wicked chuckle.

'Is that so?' asked Francesca coolly.

He grinned again. 'I do remember that much.'

'So it would seem.'

He laughed then and came and sat beside her on the sofa. 'I do believe I'm making you jealous,' he said.

'Heaven forbid. . .!'

'No, seriously, Francesca, I must admit I was concerned about Chloe. I knew I'd been dating her but that was all. I didn't know how far the relationship had gone or anything like that. . .'

'So do you know now? Was the erstwhile Sam able to fill you in on that as well?' She raised one eyebrow, and the irony of the gesture was not lost on Guy.

'Not completely.' He pulled a face. 'But he told me enough to let me know that it was me who ended the relationship.'

'Did he know why?'

'Not really. I guess Chloe came on a bit strong, pushing the marriage bit. I suppose I knew it wasn't going anywhere. Knew Chloe wasn't the woman for me, if you like, and according to Sam I finished it fairly soon afterwards.' As he spoke he reached out his hand and, taking a strand of her hair, he began twisting it around his finger.

She stiffened, longing suddenly for him to take her in his arms and tell her everything was all right. But it wasn't all right—he had phoned Chloe as well as this Sam Reynolds. He hadn't told her that, and wasn't going to by the looks of things. She took a gulp of her wine.

'Sam told me there were at least two other doctors who Chloe was involved with after me,' he said after a while, breaking into her thoughts.

'Two others?' She frowned, not understanding what he meant.

'Yes,' he nodded, 'then apparently in July, right out of the blue, Chloe suddenly married Abe Steinburg.'

Steinburg. Francesca looked up sharply. That was the name she'd heard on the answerphone, the name Chloe had given. 'Who's Abe Steinburg?' she asked carefully.

'Abe?' Guy gave a sudden chuckle. 'He's a consultant physician at the hospital where we all worked. Poor old Abe, he must be wondering what's hit him.' He shook his head, then, catching sight of Francesca's surprised expression, he explained, 'Abe was a confirmed bachelor; he lived with his widowed mother. He must be...let me see, at least twice Chloe's age...but what the hell!' He laughed out loud. 'I dare say he's happy—I only hope he'll stand the pace.' He looked at her. 'Do you know, my love?' His expression grew serious. 'I was so happy, so relieved after I'd spoken to Sam that I rang Chloe to congratulate her and Abe.'

'You did?' asked Francesca weakly.

'Yes.' He nodded. 'Sam gave me their number, but when I phoned there was nobody there. I came to bed then but you were asleep. I didn't have the heart to wake you to tell you what had happened.'

She frowned. Something still didn't seem quite right but she couldn't put her finger on what exactly. 'You rang Sam last night?' she said.

'Yes,' he replied. 'You'd gone to bed and I knew there was no point my trying to sleep—I was too disturbed. That's when I decided to ring the hospital. It was sheer luck getting Sam.'

'So did you get to sleep after that?'

'Eventually.'

She remained silent for a moment, then said, 'You weren't there this morning when I woke up. I got a call for a house visit some time around six.'

'I was awake again very early,' he admitted. 'In the end I got up and went for a walk. When I got back you'd gone out. I tried to ring Chloe and Abe again—by then it would have been about midnight their time. I thought maybe if they'd gone out for the evening they might have just got back, but the phone was still on the answering service. I guess perhaps they're away.'

'So what did you do?' She paused. 'Did you leave this number for them to call back?'

'No.' He shook his head. 'I left a message simply congratulating them and wishing them luck.' He chuckled again. 'I've got a feeling Abe's going to need it!' He paused. 'You've finished your wine—shall I get you another?'

'Sorry?' Francesca, her mind racing, stared at him as his simple explanations finally put paid to her confusion.

'Your glass,' he said softly, staring back at her, catching the emotion in her eyes but, judging by the questioning look in his own, unable to interpret it. 'It's empty. Would you like another?'

She stared down at her glass. Somewhere deep inside her some well of happiness was beginning to bubble.

She looked up at him again. 'Yes,' she said. 'Oh, yes, please.'

The following morning Francesca awoke to the sound of rain; gentle, steady rain that would wash away the dust of autumn. She lay for a long while simply listening, then carefully, so as not to disturb him, she turned her head to look at Guy.

There had been no early walk that morning and he still lay close beside her, one arm flung protectively across her body as he slept.

How could she have doubted him? She felt ashamed now that it had even entered her head that he might have been lying to her.

He looked incredibly peaceful now that his mind had been put to rest over so many of the things that had been troubling him. She also found herself wishing, just as Guy had done, that they had contacted the

States before, but at one time it had seemed as though Guy had enough to cope with in this country without possibly piling on more pressure.

They had made love again last night—a smile touched her lips at the memory—and it had been like those times in Spain, on their honeymoon, lasting far into the night as they had brought each other to the ultimate fulfilment. She loved him so much and she knew that he loved her. Even the fact that in his mind his knowledge of her only went back a few short weeks was beginning to seem insignificant as their love for each other grew.

He stirred then, yawned, and without opening his eyes rubbed a hand over the dark stubble on his jaw.

Francesca lifted her hand and gently drew a finger down his profile, the smooth forehead, the aristocratic nose, stopping, hovering then delicately tracing, outlining the sensual curve of his lips.

The next moment he'd caught her fingers between his teeth. She gasped, then laughed as he grasped her wrist in his strong fingers.

'I thought you were asleep,' she said.

'You've got to be joking,' he murmured and in a single movement rolled over, pinioning her beneath him.

'Guy,' she began to protest, 'we'll be late for work. . .'

'You shouldn't start what you don't intend finishing. . .' Releasing her wrist, he stared down, kissed the tip of her nose, then, cupping one breast in his hand, lazily caressed the nipple until it hardened in open defiance of her protests.

'We really don't have the time. . .'

'In that case, maybe we should get to the clinic——' he raised his eyebrows and stared down at her '—but I warn you, if I don't finish this now I shall just have to finish it there. . .'

She giggled.

'You think I'm joking, don't you?'

'Oh, no. No, I don't.' With an exaggerated sigh she

moved, lifting her hips to meet him. 'I know better than that,' she said in a resigned voice. 'So I suppose we'd better get on with it—I can't allow you to set a bad example to those young receptionists. Whatever would they think?'

'What indeed?' he said softly as slowly, easily he began to move. And once again, as if they'd been loving for a lifetime, they picked up the rhythm of their love.

The call came through as they took a quick breakfast of toast and coffee.

Em had died in the early hours of the morning.

'I'll be in very soon, Maureen.' Francesca replaced the receiver and turned to Guy.

'Em?' he asked. She nodded. He sighed. 'Poor Percy,' he said simply, 'he'll miss the Duchess.'

'He'll still tend his flowers for her,' remarked Francesca.

She stopped at Peacehaven on the way to the clinic in order to certify the death. The house seemed unnaturally quiet as the other residents stayed in their rooms longer than usual, prolonging the moment when they would have to confront Em's empty chair in the lounge.

'She was a wonderful character,' said Maureen as she saw Francesca to the front door; 'we'll all miss her.'

It was in a subdued mood that Francesca drove to the clinic. It always affected her when one of her patients died, whatever the circumstances of the death. Once, when she'd mentioned this to her father, saying she wished she could get used to it, his reply had been that the day she was unaffected by losing someone would be the day she stopped caring.

When she walked into the clinic she saw Guy in the open doorway of Ros's office. As he turned and caught sight of her he smiled, then said, 'The fax from Sam Reynolds is just coming through.'

As Francesca approached the office Ros tore off the sheets of paper and handed them to Guy.

'Looks as if you've got plenty to gen up on there.' Francesca smiled. 'You'd better get a move-on.'

'There's plenty of time,' said Guy, calmly taking the sheets from Ros and beginning to read them.

'You do know visitors' clinic is at eleven today?' asked Francesca casually.

'What?' Guy looked up sharply.

'Visitors,' she repeated. 'Eleven o'clock today.'

'I thought it was at three!' He stared from her to Ros, whose nod merely confirmed the fact.

Muttering to himself, Guy went off to his consulting-room, and Francesca grinned at Ros. 'He needed something to make him get his act together this morning,' she said wickedly.

'I heard that!' Guy shouted over his shoulder.

'You were meant to,' Francesca retorted and winked at Ros.

'Whatever's going on?' Ros looked bewildered.

'Nothing.' Francesca laughed. 'Really, nothing. Just our fun.'

'Oh, well, that's all right, then.' Ros looked relieved. 'If it's fun I'm all for it. I must say I thought Guy was looking much happier this morning. . .'

'Oh, he is,' agreed Francesca drily.

'Anything to do with that fax from America?' asked Ros curiously.

'Well, yes. . .partly.' Francesca paused. 'It's a long story. . .but yes. . .I think things are beginning to sort themselves out for Guy.'

'Well, I'm glad. It's not before time.'

Ros turned to her word-processor and Francesca was about to move away to her own room when she stopped, hesitated, then said, 'I don't want this to sound insensitive, Ros, but there will be a room at Peacehaven now.'

'Yes. . .' Ros frowned and bit her lip.

'Would you like me to have a word with Maureen Fellows for you?'

'I. . .I'm not sure.'

'I think it's time, Ros,' Francesca went on gently.

'You won't be able to manage for much longer. Your mum will soon be needing more care than you are able to give her. Think about it,' she added, 'but don't take too long. These things have to be decided quickly, you know that.'

'Yes, I know...' Ros took a deep breath. 'Thank you, I will think about it and I'll let you know later today.'

Francesca didn't see Guy again until lunchtime, by which time George Billows had long gone.

'So how did it go this time?' she asked, pausing as she passed the open door of his room.

He was sitting behind his desk, leaning back in his leather chair, toying with a pencil and staring out of the window. He didn't look up, hadn't appeared to hear her.

Curiously she stepped back, then, tapping on the open door with the backs of her fingers, she came right into the room.

'Hello?' she called half jokingly. 'Is there anyone at home?'

He did look up then, but even when he did see her and realise it was her she saw there was a strange expression on his face.

'What is it, Guy?' Automatically she closed the door behind her. Past experience warned her that this could be another mood swing with yet more frustration. She fervently hoped not; he had seemed so happy last night and again this morning. 'Have you seen George?' she asked tentatively.

'What?' He frowned.

'George. George Billows. Did he come to see you?'

'Oh, yes. Yes, he came.' He nodded then and swivelled his chair round to face her.

'So what happened? Did you manage to get your way through the manipulation?'

'Yes.' He nodded then appeared to hesitate. 'Well, no,' he went on after a moment, 'it wasn't quite like that.'

'What do you mean?' She stared at him, suddenly

intrigued by the look in his eyes, then realising it was a look of suppressed excitement.

'It was the most extraordinary thing,' he said slowly.

'Tell me.' She perched on the edge of the desk.

He didn't answer immediately, continuing to play with the pencil that he held balanced between his fingers, then at last, reflectively, he said, 'I studied the fax printout first.'

'Yes?' she said eagerly.

'I didn't think it told me very much.' He hesitated before continuing. 'It merely outlined the technique used...the pressure used on each vertebra...that sort of thing, and I didn't think that when I came to do the manipulation it would be much different from the first occasion, when I really ended up simply doing a massage.'

'Go on.' She leaned forward, her interest growing.

'Well, when the point came that I was actually confronted with George's back and I started the treatment, like I said, the most extraordinary thing happened. It was as if...' he paused '...as if the movements of my hands were detached in some way from the dictates of my brain.'

She stared at him. 'Do you mean you actually carried out the manipulation?'

'Yes.'

'So did you remember how to do it?'

'Not exactly. No, I don't think so.' He shook his head, still apparently bewildered by what had happened. 'I can't explain it. I don't think my mind actually remembered, but it was as if my hands instinctively did what they had been taught to do.'

'I wonder if that's what would happen if you were to go skiing?' she asked excitedly.

'I don't know.' He shrugged. 'I suppose I could find I still know how to do it; on the other hand I suppose I could end up having a nasty accident...'

'Which just might restore your memory!'

They stared at each other, then Guy burst out laughing and when she joined in he said, 'Well, at least I can laugh about it now. And talk about it, without getting screwed up.'

'I think it's still glimpses you're getting,' she said quietly, 'glimpses behind that curtain. One day, you may find it'll lift completely.'

'Maybe.' He stood up and ruefully smiled down at her. 'And maybe not. But I guess if it doesn't, it won't be the end of the world.'

One evening, towards the end of October, as they were clearing up at the end of the day Francesca walked out of her consulting-room and found Guy in Reception talking to David. She was just in time to hear David say, 'It's going to take time, but we're getting there,' before he disappeared into Ros's office.

Guy turned then and when he caught sight of her smiled and said, 'All finished?'

'More or less.' She allowed her gaze to meet his, her eyes echoing the anticipation she saw there.

'Ready for home, then?'

'Not quite,' she said. 'I have a biopsy result for Jean Blake.'

'Are you going to phone it through?'

'No.' She paused and when Guy raised his eyebrows she said, 'I thought I would go and see her.'

'That's up at Sky Fell, isn't it?'

'Yes.' She paused, then nodded towards Ros's door. 'Is everything all right?'

'Yes, I think so. Why do you ask?'

'When I came through I overheard David say something about it taking time but that they were getting somewhere. I just wondered what he meant.'

'Oh, that.' Guy smiled. 'Apparently Ros is still a bit upset about her mother going into Peacehaven. David was simply saying it was going to take time for her to adjust.'

'Do you think everything's going to be all right between those two?'

Guy grinned and nodded. 'I don't just think, I *know*

it is, in spite of old David being a bit slow on the uptake at the beginning. He's being an absolute tower of strength to Ros at the present time.'

'Well, I'm glad to hear it,' Francesca said. 'It's about time Ros had a taste of being looked after herself——' She stopped as the door of Malcolm's consulting-room suddenly opened. Lauren Richardson in her wheelchair accompanied by her mother came out of the room, closely followed by Malcolm.

'Hello!' Lauren's face, peeping from beneath the brim of a black velvet hat, lit up as she caught sight of Guy.

'Hello!' He crouched down beside her. 'So how was Disney World?' he asked. 'Did you see Mickey?'

'Yes.' The little girl beamed in excitement.

'Did you speak to him?'

'Yes.' She giggled. 'I shouted out. Mickey was in a parade, but he saw me and he came over.'

'So what did he say?'

'He asked how I was feeling. I told him sometimes I feel good and other times I feel bad. . .then I told him about you. I said you were my friend and that you and some other doctors had taken some children to see him, children from Honeysuckle House. Was that right?' Her eyes shone as Guy nodded. 'Children just like me,' she went on excitedly, 'who can't walk.'

'I hope you told him I couldn't walk after all those miles I did on that sponsored walk.'

Lauren giggled again, an infectious sound that rippled round Reception. 'I told him you got lots of blisters,' she said. 'But. . .guess what!' She looked triumphant. 'He remembered you!'

'Did he, now?' Guy smiled. 'He's a very clever mouse, isn't he?'

'I don't think he's a real mouse,' whispered Lauren solemnly.

'Really?' Guy looked shocked. 'What makes you think that?'

'Well, there was a cat in the parade,' said Lauren solemnly, 'a big cat, and Mickey wasn't even scared.

If he was a real mouse he would have been scared, wouldn't he?'

Francesca, watching and listening to the little group in the doorway, wasn't quite sure when the realisation dawned on her. The first thing she was really aware of was a sort of sixth sense and a tingle that ran the length of her spine. Then, as Malcolm helped Lauren's mother with the wheelchair, she turned to Guy.

'Will you come up to the Blakes' with me?' she said softly.

'Of course.' He followed her outside. 'Your car or mine?' he asked.

'I think,' she said thoughtfully, 'the Land Rover might be more appropriate.'

'The Land Rover?' He looked surprised. 'I know it's got a bit colder today, but I don't think we're going to have any snow.' He laughed but didn't comment further as she led the way across the car park and unlocked the vehicle.

The sun was setting, casting evening shadows across the countryside as they climbed out of Bletchley Bridge and took the high road over the fells.

'Am I with you for moral support?' asked Guy as the chimneys of Sky Fell Farm eventually came into view.

'Moral support?' Francesca threw him a quick glance, resisting, for the moment, the urge to put into words the excitement that was beginning to grip her.

'Yes. Do I gather you have bad news for Jean Blake and you fear Jeff's reaction?'

'No.' She shook her head. 'On the contrary. Jean's cervical biopsy was negative—she's in the clear. I just thought it would be nice to be the bearer of good tidings for once. Oh, and I also thought I would quietly suggest to Jeff that it might be an appropriate time to be thinking of taking Jean away on holiday.'

'So did you ask me along just for company?' He smiled. 'Not that I'm complaining, mind. . .'

'No, Guy,' she said softly. 'I didn't ask you just for your company, nice as that is.' Checking her driving mirror and ignoring his surprised glance, she pulled off the road and into a lay-by above the farm; then she switched off the engine. 'I brought you with me for a reason.'

'Tell me more.' He grinned and settled back in his seat, folding his arms.

'You haven't realised, have you?' she said, reaching out her hand and tenderly pushing back the wing of fair hair that had fallen across his forehead.

'Realised? Realised what?' He looked mystified.

She continued to watch him, loving him, loving every feature, every expression, every mannerism; then she took a deep breath. 'Back there,' she said quietly, 'don't you know what happened. . .with Lauren?'

'Lauren?' He looked puzzled, then shook his head.

'You mentioned her trip to Disney World.'

'Yes. . .'

'You remembered she'd been, Guy.'

He frowned. 'I knew she'd been, certainly. . .'

'You knew a lot about her, and she isn't your patient.'

'I knew she had been poorly since her return and I knew she is now in remission, but I'm sure I've heard others mention all this. . .'

'Yes, that's true,' she agreed patiently, 'but you also knew all the circumstances of the trip. . .details of the sponsored walk to raise money to send her to Florida. . .even the fact that you'd told her to talk to Mickey Mouse. . . Guy, those things happened before we were married. . .you've remembered them!' She could barely contain her excitement now.

'Oh, my God. . .' He stared at her in bewilderment, then as what she was saying finally sank in he passed a hand over his head, drawing it down to cover his face.

'Guy,' she whispered after a few moments, 'are you all right?'

'I'm not sure,' he said shakily, moving his hand, looking at her through his fingers. 'I hadn't realised I'd remembered that. I hadn't realised it had happened during that period of time. . .'

'I didn't think you had.'

'Why didn't you say. . .before. . .back there?'

'I didn't want to shock you too much—not in front of the others.'

He fell silent, obviously battling with his thoughts, while Francesca waited patiently.

'I don't know,' he said at last, 'whether I can recall anything else.' Then almost frantically he began to look around him, at the lakes far below, darkening now in the gathering autumn twilight, at the sheep cropping the grass beyond the rough stone walls, at a light shining in the window of Sky Fell Farm.

'It's all a muddle,' he muttered, 'I'm not sure what I've remembered and what I've been told. . .'

'Guy——' leaning forward, Francesca took both his hands and held them tightly '—look at me. That's right. Now tell me: have you been here before? To Sky Fell Farm?'

'Yes,' he answered immediately. 'When Jeff Blake had his heart attack, when the weather was so atrocious. . .when you very nearly ran me over. . . then we drove past here on our way to Carlisle when I thought it was snowing again. . .when you told me to tell Robert Carstairs. . .' He trailed off and stared at her. 'Why are you looking at me like that?' he said, then as it slowly dawned on him what he'd said he closed his eyes and let his head fall forward on to Francesca's shoulder.

It was quite dark when they got back to the cottage after seeing Jean Blake and returning the Land Rover to the clinic. Francesca barely had time to close the front door before Guy swept her into his arms, held her tightly and brought his lips down on to hers in a long kiss.

'I don't know how you've coped with me,' he said at last when they drew apart.

'Because you're my husband, because I wanted you back, and because I love you,' she said simply.

'Thank God you do,' he said. 'Heaven only knows what would have happened to me without your love and patience.' He shook his head. 'I don't think everything has come back yet,' he said haltingly.

'But it's started...it's well on the way,' she replied happily. 'I have no doubt that you'll have total recall in time.'

'The amazing part is that it happened when I was least expecting it,' he said, then added, 'And what's more, I didn't even realise it.'

'And just to think it was little Lauren who was the trigger in the end,' Francesca said quietly. She fell silent for a moment then, hardly daring to ask, she said tentatively, 'Do you remember our wedding-day?'

'I'm not sure...' He hesitated. 'I think I do, but I may be confusing the images with the photographs.'

'I'll talk you through it if you like, step by step; maybe that will help,' she replied, stretching up and kissing him lightly.

'I'm not too sure about our wedding night either,' he said solemnly. 'I think you'll need to take me through that step by step as well.' As he spoke he took her hand and began to draw her towards the stairs.

'Guy Sinclair, you are impossible,' she protested.

'Are you complaining?' He raised his eyebrows but the innocence of the question was belied by the mischief in his eyes.

'Not at all,' she replied, 'but first I have a telephone call to make.'

'Oh? A patient?' he asked.

'No, not a patient,' she replied, picking up the telephone receiver and opening her address book, 'a doctor.'

'A doctor?' He had started to climb the stairs but he paused and looked down at her.

'Yes,' she said softly as she began to dial a number, 'I think Helen Ryder should be the first to know what's happening, don't you?'

'Of course,' he smiled, 'tell her we shall see her just as soon as we can get away again.'

'Will we?' She glanced up at him in surprise.

'Of course; we have a honeymoon to complete.'

'But we only missed a couple of days at the most.'

'A lot can be achieved in a couple of days. . .'
'Guy. . .!'
'Francesca?'
'What?' She looked up at him as he leaned over the banisters.
'Don't take all night with that phone call,' he said softly. 'I have a lot of catching up to do.'

MILLS & BOON

Affairs to REMEMBER

Stories of love you'll treasure forever...

Popular Australian author Miranda Lee brings you a brand new trilogy within the Romance line—
Affairs to Remember.

Based around a special affair of a lifetime, each book is packed full of sensuality with some unusual features and twists along the way!

This is Miranda Lee at her very best.

Look out for:

A Kiss To Remember in February '96
A Weekend To Remember in March '96
A Woman To Remember in April '96

Available from WH Smith, John Menzies, Volume One, Forbuoys, Martins, Woolworths, Tesco, Asda, Safeway and other paperback stockists.

MILLS & BOON

Today's Woman

Mills & Boon brings you a new series of seven fantastic romances by some of your favourite authors. One for every day of the week in fact and each featuring a truly wonderful woman who's story fits the lines of the old rhyme 'Monday's child is…'

Look out for Eva Rutland's *Private Dancer* in January '96.

Tuesday's child Terri Thompson is certainly full of grace but will that be enough to win the love of journalist Mark Denton—a man intent on thinking the worst of her?

Available from WH Smith, John Menzies, Volume One, Forbuoys, Martins, Woolworths, Tesco, Asda, Safeway and other paperback stockists.

MILLS & BOON

Landon's Legacy

Don't miss our great new series within the Romance line…

Landon's Legacy

One book a month focusing on each of the four members of the Landon family—three brothers and one sister—and the effect the death of their father has on their lives.

You won't want to miss any of these involving, passionate stories all written by Sandra Marton.

Look out for:

An Indecent Proposal in January '96
Guardian Groom in February '96
Hollywood Wedding in March '96
Spring Bride in April '96

Cade, Grant, Zach and Kyra Landon—four people who find love and marriage as a result of their legacy.

Available from WH Smith, John Menzies, Volume One, Forbuoys, Martins, Woolworths, Tesco, Asda, Safeway and other paperback stockists.

GET 4 BOOKS AND A MYSTERY GIFT

FREE

Return this coupon and we'll send you 4 Love on Call novels and a mystery gift absolutely FREE! We'll even pay the postage and packing for you.

We're making you this offer to introduce you to the benefits of Reader Service: FREE home delivery of brand-new Love on Call novels, at least a month before they are available in the shops, FREE gifts and a monthly Newsletter packed with information.

Accepting these FREE books and gift places you under no obligation to buy, you may cancel at any time, even after receiving just your free shipment. Simply complete the coupon below and send it to:

MILLS & BOON READER SERVICE, FREEPOST, CROYDON, SURREY, CR9 3WZ.

No stamp needed

Yes, please send me 4 free Love on Call novels and a mystery gift. I understand that unless you hear from me, I will receive 4 superb new titles every month for just £1.99* each postage and packing free. I am under no obligation to purchase any books and I may cancel or suspend my subscription at any time, but the free books and gifts will be mine to keep in any case. (I am over 18 years of age)

1EP6D

Ms/Mrs/Miss/Mr _____

Address _____

_____

_____ Postcode _____

Offer closes 31st July 1996. We reserve the right to refuse an application. *Prices and terms subject to change without notice. Offer only valid in UK and Ireland and is not available to current subscribers to this series. **Readers in Ireland please write to:** P.O. Box 4546, Dublin 24. Overseas readers please write for details.

You may be mailed with offers from other reputable companies as a result of this application. Please tick box if you would prefer not to receive such offers. ☐

mps MAILING PREFERENCE SERVICE

MILLS & BOON

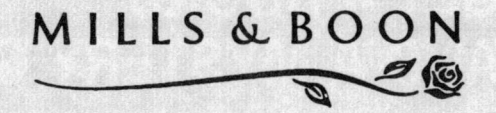

LOVE ON CALL

The books for enjoyment this month are:

PRESCRIPTION FOR CHANGE	Sheila Danton
REMEDY FOR PRIDE	Margaret Holt
TOTAL RECALL	Laura MacDonald
PRACTICE IN THE CLOUDS	Meredith Webber

Treats in store!

Watch next month for the following absorbing stories:

A FRESH DIAGNOSIS	Jessica Matthews
BOUND BY HONOUR	Josie Metcalfe
UNEXPECTED COMPLICATIONS	Joanna Neil
CRUISE DOCTOR	Stella Whitelaw

Available from W.H. Smith, John Menzies, Volume One, Forbuoys, Martins, Woolworths, Tesco, Asda, Safeway and other paperback stockists.

Readers in South Africa - write to:
IBS, Private Bag X3010, Randburg 2125.